Spider Attack!

The mountain spiders came up the ridge, fanned out in a semicircle, blocking any escape. Lan Martak stood with his back against a cliff of cold stone. A fire spell was impossible. His only chance—near suicide—was a raging river five hundred feet below.

The spiders were closing in. Lan could hear the sounds of their mandibles clicking.

He dove into empty space . . .

IRON TONGUE

ROBERT E. VARDEMAN

ACE SCIENCE FICTION BOOKS
NEW YORK

IRON TONGUE

An Ace Science Fiction Book / published by arrangement with
the author

PRINTING HISTORY
Ace Original / February 1984

ISBN: 0-441-37366-6

Ace Science Fiction Books are published by The Berkley Publishing Group,
200 Madison Avenue, New York, New York 10016.
PRINTED IN THE UNITED STATES OF AMERICA

CHAPTER ONE

"Where is he?" dark-haired, fiery-eyed Inyx demanded of Knoton. "Where is Alberto Silvain?"

"The human leader of the grey soldiers?" If metal shoulders could have shrugged, Knoton's would have done so. The mechanical's expression defied interpretation, but the way the body canted forward indicated an intense desire to discover their adversary's location. "I have patrols out looking into every room of this palace. If he is within the walls, he'll be found. We look most of all for the Lord."

Lan Martak limped in and sat heavily on an ornately carved ash footstool. The way Knoton stared at him told Lan how bad he actually looked. He felt worse. If someone had reached inside and ripped his heart out, he couldn't have been in a more debilitated state. The use of magic had pushed him beyond the limits of his endurance. Being cast into the Lord's maze had almost killed him. The long fight to regain freedom had taken a further toll. And now he had to perform still another task: finding Alberto Silvain.

"The Lord of the Twistings isn't a concern any longer. He will never again trouble you." The mechanical seemed inclined to doubt the human's opinion, but

1

Lan was too tired to argue. What little strength he still possessed had to be saved for the battle to be joined all too soon. "But Silvain is another matter. He poses an immediate threat."

"Impossible."

"With Claybore backing him, the threat is incalculable," continued Lan. He fought blacking out, wondered if it were worth the effort not slipping into Lethe. "Claybore conquers entire worlds. As he regains his body's parts and reconstructs himself, his power grows. The Lord of the Twistings was a powerful mage. He blended magic with the mechanical wondrously well, but Claybore is more powerful. He controls energies we cannot begin to comprehend."

Lan Martak let out a long, low sigh and felt the blanketing darkness creeping over him. He fought it off as long as he could. Silvain was the sorcerer Claybore's chief assistant. Eliminate him and Claybore's plans would be dealt a severe setback. But the effort of controlling his body—and holding back the fear and dread he had of Claybore—became too much. Sweet oblivion took him. Lan succumbed to the warmth of that embrace.

"Silvain is still within the palace," said Lan Martak. "Where, I can't say. But he's waiting for something."

"The cenotaph," spoke up Krek. The more-than-man-high giant spider towered over his human companions. Bouncing slightly on his coppery-furred legs, the huge arachnid appeared ready to jump. While Inyx and Lan were used to him, Knoton was not. The mechanical kept his distance from the ferocious-appearing beast. "You remember the one we 'felt' yesterday?" Krek reminded Lan.

"Yesterday?" Lan sat upright, momentarily dizzy. "I've been asleep for an entire day?"

"A bit less. The cenotaph opened and closed. Perhaps he waits for it again."

"Why do you seek a cenotaph?" asked Knoton, overcoming his distaste for the spider enough to question the humans. "What has this to do with finding Silvain?"

"A magically endowed cenotaph," explained Inyx, "allows us passage from world to world. Claybore has regained the Kinetic Sphere—his heart. He can walk the Road at will; we must use less sure paths opened by others."

"Friend Lan Martak is able to open cenotaphs for us to walk," said Krek. The huge spider clacked his mandibles in a menacing fashion. Knoton tried unsuccessfully to ignore him.

"You appear to be the match for these interlopers," said Knoton, eyeing Lan dubiously. The young adventurer looked the worse for his experiences. Learning magics in the Twistings had sapped his mental vitality, and battles with the Lord of this world had added cuts and abrasions to his body.

"Where's the graveyard?" Lan demanded of Knoton. "I sense the openings and closings, but I'm too weak to pinpoint the exact cenotaph he'll use."

"I know where it is. I have not been slumbering away my life while desperate characters like this Silvain rush about uncaptured."

"Take me there. Let's all get there. Don't waste time!" Lan cursed to himself all the way out of the palace and toward the back lawns. Inyx had to give him more support than he'd have liked. He vowed that the first thing he'd do when all this was behind them was rest for a week, then spend another week with Inyx in more enjoyable pursuits.

Afterward. . . .

He cursed the burdens placed upon him. Stopping Claybore from seizing power in every world along the Cenotaph Road was a duty better suited to a mage trained for the task, a mage as powerful as the legendary Terrill. Lan Martak had begun on a pastoral world that was just developing the magical contrivances that abounded on so many other worlds. He had grown up hunting, finding peace and tranquility in nature, depending on his strong arm and steady nerve for a living. But that was all past. Now Lan Martak got pulled deeper and deeper into the vortex of incomprehensible magics swirling between worlds. Where once he had used simple fire-starting spells to cook dinner, now he wrought magics able to smash armies and send entire planets spinning crazily into their suns.

He alone of those adventurous souls walking the Cenotaph Road had the power and ability to stop Claybore from reconstructing his scattered body and becoming the greatest despot of myriad histories.

They made their way out onto the neatly cropped lawn, down the path and toward a small stand of trees. From this close, Lan "saw" the cenotaph—or cenotaphs. No fewer than eight neatly tended crypts clustered in this minuscule graveyard.

"I've never seen so many in one place."

"Nor I," agreed the spider. "This is a world of strange contrasts. Obviously great courage is possible. Perhaps that goes with great evil, also."

"What are these cenotaphs?" asked Knoton. "You humans speak of them as if they were the most marvelous things in the world."

How could flesh and blood ever explain the concept of death to a mechanical? Or was it possible that mechs recognized disassembly in the same way? Lan didn't have the energy to explore the topic at the moment.

"They open gateways to other worlds by tapping the spirits of those dead but never properly interred. Using the Kinetic Sphere—his heart—Claybore walks the Cenotaph Road at will now, collecting hidden body artifacts. Silvain and others aid him; we oppose them."

"Succinctly put," came Alberto Silvain's words. Lan

spun, reaching for a magical death tube at his belt. His hand froze halfway there when he saw that Silvain aimed one of the weapons directly at Inyx's head. The commandant of Claybore's grey-clad troops laughed, saying, "So it's as I surmised. You'd face your own death willingly enough to stop me—and Claybore. But you won't risk her life. Claybore will find that interesting."

"You know what he's trying to do," said Lan, trying to find the most convincing words. "Join us, oppose him."

"I side with winners."

"Like the not very lamented Lord of the Twistings?" asked Krek, his voice curiously mild and childlike for a creature so large.

"I had no choice in his case. Claybore ordered me to support him. Given the chance, I would have removed him permanently. I see that our lovely Inyx did that and more. She has a ruthlessness in her that I admire."

"I'd rip out your liver and stuff it down your throat, if I could," the woman said, her tone low and menacing. She jerked against the man's strong forearm, held in a bar across her throat. Attempting to sink teeth into his flesh availed her little. He turned just enough to prevent any damage.

"See? Such an admirable display of courage. Too bad I must kill you all before joining Claybore."

"He's not doing too well regaining his tongue." Lan made it a statement, not a question.

"How'd you know . . . Ah, a trick. There is no way you can know what happens on that world. You don't even know which world he's on. But as you have already learned from me in a careless moment, yes, progress is much too slow. I am now free of this world and can aid him. Then I shall return to this world and make it my own personal domain. He's promised me."

"The cenotaph opens," said Krek.

Alberto Silvain jerked slightly in his eagerness to

leave behind the world of his defeat. Inyx ducked, pulled free, then rolled behind a gravestone. The death beam lashed out and blew the marker into tiny stone fragments. Silvain poised for a second shot when he saw Knoton, Krek, and Lan simultaneously starting for him. The odds were too great, the need to escape this world too binding.

He dived into the already opened crypt just inches under Lan's death beam.

Even as they approached, Lan Martak knew they were too late to stop the transition. Krek made a tiny choking noise, then sat down, legs akimbo around him.

"He is gone," lamented the spider. "He has walked the Cenotaph Road."

"It'll be a full day before we can follow, too. Curse the luck!"

"You would follow?" Knoton asked, in surprise. "But if the other side is like this one, why can't Silvain post a guard who will kill you as you emerge?"

"No reason in this world—or any world. We have to try to stop him, though. Claybore's evil makes the Lord of the Twistings look puny in comparison."

The mechanical said nothing, studying the two humans and their arachnid companion.

"It opens at any moment," said Krek, peering into the open crypt.

"How are we going to do this?" asked Inyx. "Claybore and Silvain are sure to have their soldiers waiting for us."

"Time flows differently between worlds. We might be able to arrive closely enough on Silvain's heels that he hasn't had time to contact Claybore."

"A faint hope."

"Yes," Lan Martak admitted. "But still a hope." He and Inyx stood, arms around one another. The cenotaph began to glow a pale, wavering sea-green, to open its gateway onto a new world. Lan glanced at his companions. Krek's expression was as spiderish and indecipherable as ever, but a clacking of his mandibles revealed an almost-human nervousness at what lay ahead. Under his arm, Inyx shivered, but Lan knew it was more excitement than fear on the woman's part. She came from a warrior-world; while she might know fear on a secret level, it seldom surfaced to show its pale face to others. For himself, he was too exhausted to feel anything but the weight of duty—and destiny.

Lan, Inyx, and Krek crowded forward to squeeze into the cenotaph on their way to find and kill Silvain and his master, Claybore.

The transition from one world to another disoriented Lan, as it always did. He might walk the Road for a million years and still not become fully acclimated to the giddy turnings and mind-wrenchings of this magical travel.

"Friend Lan Martak," he heard Krek saying. Lan shook his head, as if to clear the haze from his brain. It didn't help; it only hurt. Fire bugs chewed through his insides and something kicked unmercifully at the backs of his eyes.

"Lan," came another, softer, more urgent voice. He forced open his eyes to peer up and out of the cenotaph at Inyx. The woman stood above him, long, slender legs widespread, hands on her flaring hips. Her attention wasn't on him but on something at some distance.

Lan took a deep breath and tasted the wet sweetness of nearby lush vegetation. But undercutting it came a new scent, one he had seldom encountered. This was definitely not the world of the Twistings. That world abounded with fresh growth. Here, the plant life seemed . . . abbreviated.

The man heaved himself out of the opened grave and followed Inyx's extended arm. He took in the tiny area around them. Here grew thick grasses and towering plants with stems as thick as his wrist. Just beyond, hardly a bowshot distant, some brutal demarcation had been drawn between life and death. Green, growing life ended and hot sterile sands triumphed. But it was beyond even this ring that Inyx pointed.

"A caravan ambushed by the grey-clads," she said.

Lan squinted in harsh sun and nodded. The scene proved all too familiar for him. On world after world, the grey-clad soldiers commanded by Claybore and his underlings conquered, killing without quarter, seizing power, crushing all dissent.

It happened here, also.

Tired to the core of his being, Lan still drew forth his sword and nodded to his companions. They had not come here to rest. They must fight. And what better side to take than of those already knowing the terror and death brought by Claybore's rule?

"Aieeeee!" shrieked Krek, his long legs extending to their fullest. The spider charged, death scythes clacking ominously even as his shrill keening echoed forth.

Lan and Inyx were only a few paces behind. Lan's death tube bounced at his side, but he ignored it, for the moment. The adrenaline pumping through his arteries filled him with bloodlust. The smooth stroke of his sword, the meaty feel of it striking home, the jarring all the way to his shoulder, those were the sensations he now sought.

He found them quickly.

The battle welled up around him like artesian waters. Lan parried, hacked, riposted, thrust. He fell into old, practiced routines that had served him well in the past and served him admirably now. The battle had been going against the scruffy band of travelers; Claybore's soldiers were too well-equipped and trained for any roving band to easily drive off. But with two additional swords and Krek's fearsome bulk and intimidating manner of doing battle, the greys fell back to regroup.

"After them!" cried Krek.

Lan reached out and seized one of Krek's thick back legs. He was dragged a few paces before Krek's bloodlust died sufficiently for him to realize the folly of pursuit at this moment.

"I am so ashamed," the spider moaned, settling down into the sand beside Lan. "I kill wantonly. Oh my, why is it I do these awful things?"

"You were protecting these others from Claybore's men," pointed out Inyx, stroking Krek's gore-stained fur.

"But they are only humans," sniffed the spider.

"Aye, that we are," came the cautious words of one of the men. He approached, sword in hand, wary of the spider. "And glad we are that you showed when you did. Though we find it strange that the likes of you would aid us willingly."

"Do the grey-clads control much of this world?" asked Lan.

"Those dung beetles?" scoffed the man. "Hardly. We hold them off with ease."

From one of the others came a muffled snort of derision. Lan looked at the other men and women in the group. None had escaped injury. Their original number had been twenty. The brief skirmish had cost them half their rank.

"It appears you are doing all right," Lan said, testing the man's reaction. He introduced himself and his companions. The man he faced had eyes only for Inyx, who smiled at the attention.

"And I, good sir, hight Jacy Noratumi, commander of the desert reaches of the magnificent empire of Bron."

"Magnificent, he says," mocked one of the women in the band, as she held a broken arm to her belly. "Jacy is hardly more than a pirate these days. As are we all. We used to be miners, traders, honest folks earning our living in peace. Those scum drive us like

herd animals. Bron is little more than a pathetic huddling of huts hidden behind an all-too-thin wall.''

"Silence, Margora," the man snapped. Smiling, he
turned back to Lan and said, "She is always the
pessimist. We are seldom caught in such a fashion on
the sands. The dung-eating greys came upon us un-
expectedly. They rode like demons for the oasis.''

"To stop us," said Inyx, bitterness etching her voice.

"You?" asked the woman Margora suspiciously. She
glanced from Inyx to Lan. When her eyes fixed on the
brown lump near the cenotaph, she stiffened visibly.
"Jacy," she said, her voice hardly more than a whisper.
"We cannot trust one of *them*!"

Lan Martak saw the woman's response came from
finally realizing that Krek was something other than
human. In the heat of battle and the shocked interreg-
num after, there had been little enough time to do more
than slump in exhaustion. Now that the battle fury and
tiredness wore off, logical processes resumed. And the
arachnid did not arouse good feelings in any of the
natives of this world. All reached for daggers and swords,
hands restlessly stroking hilts in preparation for the
order to attack.

"Hold," said Jacy Noratumi, his voice sharp. "It is
with these, our friends." Lan noticed that the man's
shining amber eyes locked firmly on Inyx when he spoke.

Krek could not remain silent at being termed an
"it." The formless lump he had collapsed into stirred,
legs extended to propel the spider to his full height;
sand showered down on them. Krek dominated the
scene, anger returning.

"I am Webmaster of the Egrii Mountains," he said
with the cut of a sword in his usually mild voice.

"You are . . ." began Margora. But the woman's
words were drowned by the shouts of sentries.

"The grey-clads return," Noratumi said. "Our differences are to be placed aside until after we finish off our

foes.'' He indicated the approaching dust cloud that partly cloaked the mounted forms of Claybore's soldiers.

Lan moved closer to Inyx, but Jacy had already interposed himself. Lan had no chance to comment; a thundering wave of riders crashed against their pathetic defenses like a hurricane-tossed wave on a house of cards. His sword sang a bloody tune, hacking, driving, parrying, sometimes finding targets, sometimes successfully preventing an enemy's sword from finding his flesh.

Even with Krek's potent fighting ability thrown into the fray, the battle went against those on the ground.

"There, Lan, look!" came Inyx's cry. The young warrior-mage turned to see where she pointed with her gore-encrusted blade. Pounding down on them was Alberto Silvain. Lan felt magical powers welling inside, but he fought them; he had no time and couldn't afford to expend the energy needed for a proper spell.

He relied on his trusty sword. Steel flashed in the bright desert sun. A hard jolt rattled his teeth as his sword edge slashed into Silvain's horse. The blade nearly severed the right front leg just above the knee. Horse and rider cartwheeled forward, but Lan lost hold of his sword in the maelstrom of flying bodies.

Silvain hit on his shoulders and rolled smoothly, coming to his feet. He, too, had lost his sword, but not his dagger. Claybore's henchman swiftly drew his knife, lifted a brawny arm, and lunged—straight for Inyx's unprotected back.

"*Inyx!*" screamed Lan, but even as the name ripped from his throat he knew the warning could never save her. Silvain was too close, too fast, too deadly.

CHAPTER TWO

Lan Martak felt as if the world turned in jerky motions about him. The heat of the battle seemed distant, the death and blood a product of a nightmare half-remembered. Helpless to intercede, he saw Alberto Silvain pull forth a gleaming silver dagger and drive it directly for Inyx's kidney. Lan's mind worked in a frenzy, but to no avail. No spell came to his lips quickly enough to stop Silvain. No weapon was at hand. The distance was too great. Inyx would die.

"*Inyx!*" he heard, as if the warning came from another's lips. The dark-haired woman started to twist about, but had only begun the motion as Silvain drove forward with deadly intent.

Lan thought his own fervent hopes had caused him to see what he wanted to see rather than the reality of his lover's death. With Silvain fractions of an inch away from his target, a blinding silver arc swept downward, deflecting the dagger. Even through the din of battle, Lan heard the harsh grating of metal against metal. Silvain's dagger flew from his grip.

Jacy Noratumi laughed delightedly at the sight of Alberto Silvain's confusion and rage.

"So, grey shit-eater, you think to rob one so lovely

12

of her life? With a foul blow to the back? Meet me, face to face, and I shall show you true valor. For once in your miserable life you should witness it!''

Noratumi's blade swung at shoulder level, forcing Silvain to duck under or lose his head. The grey-clad officer dived, rolled, and retrieved a fallen sword. By this time, Inyx had taken in the closeness of her death and how best to prevent Silvain from again attempting it.

She swung her own blade in a low arc. Silvain had to do a quick double hop-step to avoid losing a leg. As he moved, so did Noratumi. The sallow man dashed in, blade held straight in front of him like a razor-sharp battering ram. Between Noratumi and Inyx, they kept Claybore's henchman stumbling, retreating, fighting simply to preserve his own miserable life.

Lan heaved a sigh of relief at this and went to yank his own blade free from the downed horse's leg. He planted his foot on the animal's side and yanked hard. With a tearing, grinding sound, his weapon pulled loose. He spun about to see where best his talents could be used, but the battle was quickly winding down. To his left, Krek slashed and dismembered a half-dozen of the grey-clads. The others of Jacy Noratumi's band fought with wild abandon, as if the thought of death had never occurred to them. This ferocity and selflessness forced Claybore's troops ever backward.

Amid the coppery tang of fallen blood, Lan inhaled and smelled the lushness of the oasis once again. This time it almost sickened him. The blood, the sweat of terror, the heated metal all ruined what had once been a soothing odor. He closed his eyes and let the tide of battle wash over him, past him, around him. The sounds decreased as Silvain's soldiers mounted and fled, leaving behind only Noratumi's gasping warriors. A hot breeze whipped at his tattered clothing and burned at his

skin, but Lan didn't mind that. He lived. Inyx and Krek
lived.

And so did Claybore somewhere on this world.

"Inyx!" he called, opening his eyes and peering
about. The warrior woman leaned casually on her sword,
Jacy Noratumi near by. The two talked earnestly,
Noratumi moving slightly closer every few sentences.
Lan Martak joined them.

"Thank you," he said to Noratumi.

"For what? The battle? It ought to have done us in,
but luck—or the Four Fates—were with us. I favor the
idea of luck being on our side. The Fates have not been
good to Bron's legions of late."

"Who can ever be thankful for a battle? No, I thank
you for saving her life." He looked at Inyx. The woman
had never appeared more alive, more lovely, more
desirable. The battle had brought a flush to her cheeks
and a ripe fullness to her figure. If there had ever truly
been one born to do battle, Lan knew it was Inyx. She
had lost brothers and family and walked the Road and
never once looked back on her misfortunes; she lived
by her wit and quick sword. In its way, this fighting
prowess had substituted for the lack of family by giving
her something to count on.

"I've already given my thanks, Lan," she said. Her
vivid blue eyes bored into his softer brown ones. "But
thank you for the thought."

"Milady says you are something of a sorcerer. Can
you bring back the dead?"

"What?" Lan snapped out of his reverie. The tone
Noratumi had taken in asking the question reminded
him of the woman Margora's when referring to Krek.
"I'm no necromancer. The dead remain so. Why do
you ask that question?"

"We have no love for sorcerers, either." Noratumi's
eyes lifted from Lan up and past his shoulder to where

Krek meticulously wiped himself free of the blood on thorax and legs.

"This place seems to be much divided," Lan said cautiously. "You war with spiders. You have no liking for mages. You engage the grey-clads whenever possible."

"That is an adequate summation." Noratumi moved a half-step closer to Inyx. "The sorcerers kidnap us and force us into slavery. The spiders eat us." The distaste with which he spoke was obvious. "We have no love of either. And then come these interlopers, these grey butchers. The empire of Bron stands against all three!"

Bravado, decided Lan, not answering the obvious challenge. The politics of the world did not interest him; finding and defeating Claybore was all that mattered.

"What do you know of a tongue?"

"A tongue?" From the manner in which Noratumi stiffened and moved his hand closer to his sheathed dagger, Lan knew he had touched a sore point with the man. As loath as he was to anger Noratumi, he had to find out quickly about the tongue Claybore so eagerly sought. That it was in this world Alberto Silvain had accidentally revealed; that the search went poorly for Claybore was also obvious. Lan Martak desired to aid any enemy of Claybore.

"Claybore seeks his tongue on this world," spoke up Inyx, increasingly uneasy at the tension between Lan and Jacy. "We would destroy it." Lan watched Noratumi's reaction and failed to understand the complex flood of emotions.

"Iron Tongue," was all the man said, then spun and stalked off, his knuckles white around the hilt of his sword.

"What produced such a reaction in our temporary ally?" asked Krek. The spider shook himself before burrowing down in a sandy patch and rubbing the last traces of gore from his legs. "He appears not to trust us. And after all we have done for him. Humph."

"You're right," said Inyx. "This world aligns itself strangely. The woman was frightened of you, not because of your size, but simply because you were a spider."

"All humans have this weakness. I cannot understand it myself. After all, we spiders do not instantly fear all humans. In fact, in less enlightened times, I rather enjoyed catching them in the high passes and feeding on them." The spider gusted a loud sigh. "Those were such pleasant times. But unenlightened, as I said."

Lan ignored his friend's bout with nostalgia.

"The more interesting response came when Inyx mentioned Claybore's tongue. Noratumi knows of it."

"Or," put in Inyx, "where that information can be had." Her eyes followed Jacy Noratumi as the man went from wounded to wounded, shaking his head from time to time and always trying to comfort even those with no hope of survival.

Lan Martak felt himself pulled inside as he watched her. That Inyx was attracted to Jacy was indisputable. Noratumi fought well, cut a fine, handsome figure of a man, and had an air about him that belied the obvious hard times he and his band had fallen on. None of this made the young adventurer feel any better. Lan was tired of fighting, tired of turning and seeing Claybore's men seemingly multiply even as he cut them down, tired to the bone of the magics that turned him into something other than he desired.

"Margora is dead," came Noratumi's quiet words. Lan snapped out of his stupor to stare at the man. While the simple sentence carried no inflection, the emotion underlying it ran as deep and clear as any spring-swollen river.

"You loved her?" asked Inyx.

"A warrior second to none, she was," he said. "Her loss will be sorely felt for a great, long time. But you do not need to hear of our sorrow. What do you do in this place? The Oasis of Billro is off the caravan paths normally taken—at least it is since the grey-clads destroyed Xas and Clorren last year."

"We walk the Cenotaph Road, fighting Claybore." Lan didn't wish to reveal more than he had to. While Noratumi opposed Claybore, mutual enemies did not instantly mean they were allies.

"So does Iron Tongue, and look at how he and the empire of Bron fight."

"Iron Tongue?" asked Inyx, too eagerly for Lan's comfort. He tried to silence her, to tell her that Noratumi ought not learn too much of their quest. He failed; the woman was intent on pursuing the meaning behind the name.

"He is sorcerer-leader of the city-state Wurnna."

"And he enslaves your people."

"He forces us to work in the power stone mines! Curse him! Curse all sorcerers." Noratumi's eyes bored into Lan's. It took the youth's full control learned through the myriad battles with Claybore not to flinch under the burning, accusing intensity of that stare. "Though you do not appear to be of Iron Tongue's ilk, you claim kinship."

"I claim nothing. I am not much of a sorcerer."

"That is true. He isn't much of a mage, but he learns," cut in Krek. "Why, he cannot conjure up even the simplest of meals. A grub or two would be appreciated now. Or mayhaps even a large worm. Nothing fancy, mind you, but certainly something adequate for a poor spider's meal."

"I learn magics because fighting Claybore requires it." Lan's hand moved slowly upward until it laid over the hidden grimoire he had received on a mountaintop on a world many grave markers distant. That dying mage had entrusted the secret of creating the cenotaph roadway to Lan—and placed on him the burden of pursuing and defeating Claybore. What one mage had failed at, another must accomplish. Lan Martak had been given that task.

"You do swing a sword over-well to be any necromancer I am acquainted with. Iron Tongue would never callus his hands with work," Noratumi observed. Again came the intense hatred boiling from the man like froth from a cauldron. Noratumi whirled around and said, "This eight-legged horror offends my people, who have had relatives and friends eaten by those of his kind in the mountains. You are a sorcerer and the empire of Bron is at war with Wurnna."

"But we all fight the grey-clad armies," cut in Inyx. She moved to Noratumi's side and placed her hand on his upper arm. "Let us join forces," she implored. "We are stronger united than fighting one another. Claybore is the enemy. Let us fight *him* and not each other."

Lan closed his eyes and allowed his small magical sense to expand outward. Inyx's spell was more subtle, more human than any he had learned from a grimoire, but that didn't stop it from being effective. He "felt" Jacy Noratumi's resolve against them softening just as he and Krek "felt" the presence of a cenotaph pathway between worlds. Inyx continued to ply the man with honeyed words until he curtly agreed that they might accompany him and his remaining people back to Bron.

After Noratumi stalked off, Inyx said, "He is an honorable man. I like him."

"He saved your life from Silvain. For that, I owe him eternal thanks."

Inyx frowned a bit, then turned and hurried after Noratumi. Lan trailed behind, moving more slowly. Krek clacked his mandibles together and muttered to himself, "Humans."

Lan Martak found the going difficult, but he worried most about Krek. The giant spider drank no water; all his moisture came from the insects and other creatures he ate. In the center of the burning desert, even tiny grubs were few and far between. For the humans it was a struggle but one bearable due to the casks of water filled at the oasis and carried on carts drawn by horses. The arachnid foraged constantly, but Lan saw the increasing shakiness in the long legs as Krek marched along.

"Well, old spider," he said through cracked lips, "are those shrubs worthy of attention?"

"Those?" scoffed Krek. "They contain nothing of interest."

"They smell like creosote."

"Smell? Always you taunt me with this pseudo-human condition you term *smell*. There is no such thing." The spider's tone indicated he would have crossed arms in determination if he'd possessed them. "The few petty bugs crawling about on those branches offer little for me."

"Is there no other way for you to get water?"

A ripple passed along the spider's coppery-furred legs until the entire bulk of his body shook.

"Water. It is almost as bad as fire. I do wish you would consider other conjurings, friend Lan Martak. You pull fire from your fingertips. Are you now deciding whether or not to bring down odious torrents of rain on my head? Oh why, oh why did I ever leave my precious Klawn and the sanctity of my web to wander?"

"She wanted to eat you, that's why," said Inyx.

"Of course she wanted to devour me. We had mated." Krek heaved a human-sounding sigh and added, "Why must I be so weak? Staying and allowing my hatchlings to feed off my carcass is so . . . natural."

The crunch of sand under their boot soles was the only sound reaching them. Lan found it harder and harder to speak through his parched lips. Even swallowing presented problems. But what Krek had said triggered a line of thought.

He held out his left hand, fingers spread slightly, lips barely forming the proper words. Tiny blue sparks danced from finger to finger as he conjured the simple fire spell he had learned so long ago. A small change in the magics and those sparks turned to intense jets of flame. He pondered the spell, examined the parts, and worried over the intricate fittings of one chant with another, one syllable with still another.

"What's wrong, Lan?" asked Inyx. "You're not suffering, like Krek, from the lack of water?"

"No, it's something else, something he said. If I can bring forth fire, why can't I also conjure the reverse?"

"Cold?"

"Cold," he agreed. "That would condense water from the atmosphere. I've tried producing water wells or even bringing water to the surface where we could get at it, but that's beyond my power. But *cold*—that ought to be possible."

"Work on it," the woman said, her voice telling him that she held no chance for success. "Look, here comes Jacy."

The leader of the band walked up, stride sure in spite of the sun wilting all the others. He gave Inyx a broad smile and clapped Lan on the back.

"I've spoken with my people. They have agreed to allow both you and the spider to remain with us until we reach Bron."

"I hadn't realized there was any debate. You'd said we could accompany you."

"A leader always respects the wishes of his followers. Or rather, a wise man decides what the people want, then tells them that's what he is going to do. They don't disagree—they agree. And they follow, even when other matters arise."

"Our presence was one of these 'other matters?' "

"Correct." Jacy Noratumi glanced up at Krek and said, "He was the point most debated. Some of the warriors have had relatives devoured by the mountain spiders."

"Tell me of them," Krek interjected. "I must know if they are of my clan. Of all the worlds along the Road I have seen, never have I encountered others directly related. Of course, there were those mere spiders who gave my good friend Lan Martak such a difficult time while we ambled up Mount Tartanius. They were . . ."

"Krek," Lan said sharply, silencing what might turn into a long and boring recital. "His point is well taken, though. What of these mountain arachnids? Are they exactly like Krek in size?"

"A merest hair smaller, mayhap, but that is difficult to say. Certainly no larger." Noratumi pulled forth his sword and thrust upward, stopping a hand's width away from Krek's thorax. "Yes, they are his size. I've killed enough of their number to know my distances."

"The others won't harm him, will they?" asked Inyx. "You've given your word. Will they abide by it, also?"

"Dear lady, I have given you my word, my bond, my surety. On my honor, none will break it, else they answer to me personally," Jacy replied.

Lan snorted dust from his nostrils, as much in reaction to the clogging as to Noratumi's melodramatic words and gestures accompanying them. The youth recognized that Noratumi played to an audience of one: Inyx. And he did not care for it.

The day dragged on; the burnished sun above seared skin and sucked precious moisture from their bodies. Lan idly played with the fire spell, altering it until he felt coolness rather than heat forming at his fingertips. Still not satisfied, he continued refining it until they took a break from their plodding across measureless desert sands.

Seated under a canvas canopy, he and Inyx set up a small glass flask, its narrow mouth inverted over a shallow dish. He concentrated, did the chants in a low voice, and felt the coldness forming between his hands. Placing them on the flask, he sat with eyes closed, allowing the spell to do its work.

"Lan, you're doing it!" cried Inyx. "Water is forming. Look!"

He opened his eyes, forced them into focus, and saw that the dark-maned woman spoke the truth. The chilled flask condensed moisture inside; it beaded on the glass walls, then trickled into the dish. He had accumulated a saucerful of precious water.

"So little," he muttered. "I had hoped for more."

"But Lan, it's enough to show you can do it. This is enough to keep a person from dying of thirst." She bent down and sipped at the liquid. "Hmmm, it's quite good, too. Better than the tepid slime Jacy carries in his casks."

It was small enough as compliments went, but it warmed Lan. Inyx and her enthusiasm for his accomplishment made his hardships more bearable. He leaned over and kissed her. The passion increased until Inyx pulled back and said, "Lan, not here. It . . . it's so public."

He didn't answer—with words. The rest of the encampment either slept, tossed in exhausted dreams, or were busily engaged in fixing equipment. None cared what went on under the canopy balanced between two stony outcroppings at the far edge of camp. None except Lan and Inyx. His lips stilled her protest, his body pressed into hers, and soon they were passionately engaged.

Afterward, Inyx stretched out like a feline and sighed.

"It has been so long, Lan. Since the Twistings."

"That wasn't so long ago," he pointed out. "But it certainly seems it. It was a world ago."

"New enemies, new friends," she agreed. "New dangers, also."

He followed her line of sight and saw the cause of her concern. Krek melted in with the landscape, appearing nothing more than a lumpy boulder among boulders. His entire body had become shrunken with the ordeal of marching in the summertime desert. The spider exalted in the cold heights of the mountains; heat depleted his strength far faster than it did a human's.

"He has to get out of this wasteland soon," she said.

"Noratumi says it is another week's march to Bron. I get the feeling that Bron and Wurrna are closer than that to one another, but this detour takes them far enough from the sorcerers to avoid confrontation." Lan idly ran his fingers over Inyx's sweat-sheathed body, the thrill he'd felt for her now turning to concern for Krek. "I think you're right. Krek can't last that long."

"What about the mountains yonder? They appear only a day or two distant."

Lan frowned. He had considered this, but didn't want to broach the topic. Splitting forces when they were so few wasn't wise; yet if it meant saving Krek's life he had no real choice. The mountains thrust rocky, scrub-covered foothills out into the desert to the west, while the humans pushed ever southward.

"We might reach the mountains, then skirt them until we can meet again at Bron. That route is much longer—perhaps a week longer."

"But safer for Krek. He can find food and moisture in the mountains."

Lan Martak worried over the best course of action to follow. He knew what it was and hated it the more. He finally said, "Krek and I will head for the mountains. You continue on with Noratumi and see what condition this empire of Bron is in."

"Lan, no! I'll go with you and Krek. We shouldn't split up like this."

"I wish it were possible to stay together, but someone has to stay with Noratumi, if we want his people to fight alongside us. You are the only one in our small rank that they find totally acceptable. They brand me a sorcerer and Krek, well, it is obvious about him. Rally support, find their weaknesses so we may strengthen them, find their strengths so we may best use them against Claybore."

"We should stay together," she said.

"Time is of the essence. It is dangerous dividing our forces while Silvain still patrols this area. He will not accept his defeat lightly. He will return with reinforcements—and he has probably informed Claybore of his encounter at the oasis. Claybore might decide to eliminate Bron in one quick stroke. Any such attack weakens our position."

"It hardly seems fair."

"Nothing has been fair since I first encountered Claybore's minions." Lan paused, then smiled, almost shyly. "The only good from this battle is meeting you." He bent and kissed her gently.

"I do not like Inyx going off with that brigand," Krek said petulantly. "She is one human who understands me."

"You mean I don't?" Lan Martak trudged along, forcing himself to put one foot in front of the other and not think of the heat or his own bone-jarring tiredness.

Krek didn't answer him directly. "She is a rare one, that Inyx. A true warrior. She displays a bloodthirstiness that is almost spiderlike. Admirable. Most admirable."

"That's one topic on which we agree fully. How much further is it to the foothills?" They had left Inyx with Noratumi's band of traders the day before. Lan's vision misted slightly as he watched the dust cloud stir and surround the departing humans while he and Krek

struck out at right angles and started a shorter trip to the
mountainous region paralleling the desert.

"If I were not in such a debilitated and pathetic
condition, a mere hour's travel. As it is, who can say? I
might die in this miserable place, far from my web and
loving mate. O Klawn, can you ever forgive me for my
dalliances?"

Lan thought the spider was going to begin crying. He
placed a hand on the nearest bristly, thick leg. Krek jerked
away as if touched by a firebrand.

"Sorry," said Lan. "We'll get into the mountains,
you can find some decent food, we can rest, and then
it'll be about ten days before we rejoin Inyx."

Krek stumbled and fell, legs tied into painful knots.

The man hastened to aid his friend, but Krek couldn't
stand under his own power.

"Time to stop for the day," Lan announced, as if he
were the one too exhausted to continue. "Let's get
camp set up and then we can rest until sunset. A good
start at twilight when it's cooler will get us into the
mountains before midnight."

"Leave me, friend Lan Martak. I am a shadow of my
former self. A weakling always, I now pull you into
death, also. That is something I cannot have on my
conscience."

"You've saved me from worse, old spider. This is an
easy way for me to even the score."

Lan stretched out the canvas canopy in the form of a
lean-to and began using his chilling spell to generate a
mouthful of drinking water for himself. The spell required little of his precious energy and supplied a product he desperately needed. His mouth felt as if it were
filled with cotton and swallowing became a painful
chore. Jacy Noratumi hadn't allowed Lan any of the
water from his casks, claiming they'd need it more and
that a single day's travel without water wouldn't harm
the young sorcerer. Lan's pride had prevented him from

arguing the point. Now his cooling spells proved useful.

Two mouthfuls of water; then he fell into an unconsciousness closer to a coma than sleep.

With the trance came visions, dreams, nightmares. And superimposed on all was a fleshless death's skull with gleaming ruby beams lancing forth from sunken eye sockets. Those beams turned and twisted and sought Lan's body until the skull smiled and began to laugh.

Lan Martak awoke with a start, his body drenched in sweat, a single name on his lips: "Claybore!"

He sat, legs pulled up and arms circling them, until it was twilight and time to push on toward the mountains.

CHAPTER THREE

"They will be all right. The spider is stronger than he lets on and the man, well, the man is a sorcerer. They can walk through walls. No harm will come to them." Jacy Noratumi placed his hand lightly on Inyx's shoulder. The woman flinched away.

How could he possibly know how she felt about Lan Martak and the big, ugly, furry, gentle-savage spider?

"I do not wish to see them leave like this. Splitting our forces only invites trouble. Alberto Silvain still patrols the area."

"Silvain, ha!" cried Noratumi, making a flourish in the air with his free hand. "He dares nothing after we so soundly defeated him at the oasis." In a different tone, almost crafty, he asked, "What do you know of this Silvain? Of all Claybore's assistants, I have never seen him before."

"We chased him along the Road. He had almost complete power on another world, and we drove him off."

"You did?"

She looked sharply at the man, seeking any sign of mockery. She didn't find it.

"I helped. Much of it was Lan's doing. For all his

protestations, he is becoming a fine mage. Claybore had trapped me between worlds in a ghostly whiteness. Lan rescued me, something others claimed impossible." She didn't elaborate, telling Noratumi she believed the task had become possible due to her love for Lan reaching out and finding him at the proper instant—and Lan's love for her powering the spells needed to lever her free of the white nothingness.

"You do battle on a grander scale."

Again she sought even a hint of irony and found nothing but simple statement.

"We have tracked Claybore across three planets. In the Twistings, we defeated him. On top of Mount Tartanius, the victory was a bittersweet one. We prevented his expansion into that world, but he regained torso and heart."

"You've seen him?"

"Aye." She shivered in spite of the heat beating down upon her. "When first we crossed swords, he was nothing more than a fleshless skull toted about in a wooden box. Now he has joined head to torso and heart, can travel at will between the worlds, and even has a magically powered mechanical acting as his legs."

"Then the myths contain more truth than any of Bron imagined." Noratumi and Inyx walked side by side, hips brushing. "We have heard how his body was scattered along the Road, but who could give credence to such a wild tale told to amuse and frighten children?"

"It is all too true. It has come down to Lan, Krek, and me to stop him. Somehow, we find ourselves uniquely suited to the task, though none of us really wanted to become involved in such madness."

"It is a dangerous goal. Claybore's troops overrun this world and have destroyed all but a few small cities. Wurrna—curse all sorcerers!—survives, as does my Bron. But the others? Gone. We were traders. There is no one left to trade with. We mine ores and work the metals. The mines are closed to us by the spiders, except when a Wurrna mage enslaves one of us and forces us into their mines.''

''You and the others ought not to fight among yourselves. Unite and fight the common threat, then work out your differences when Claybore is no longer interested in this world.''

Noratumi laughed, the bellowing laughter coming from deep inside. He shook his head, wiped at tears and sent rivers of sweat cascading off his sallow face.

''You make it sound so easy. Iron Tongue would torture me with a thousand hideous spells, should he trap me unawares. And the spiders? I'd sooner give myself gladly to Iron Tongue rather than enter their valley. I have no liking for your puppet-mage, but I do not envy him accompanying the spider into *those* hills.'' He looked up and away at the rocky ridge toward which Lan and Krek had started.

''He is not my 'puppet-mage,' '' she snapped.

''A thousand pardons if I have offended, milady.'' Noratumi made a courtly bow. This time Inyx detected the sneer in his tone. ''I do not gladly suffer any mage in my midst, no matter who accompanies him.''

Inyx shook her long, dark hair in a wide-swinging fan pattern. The sunlight caught strands and sent out tiny rainbows of color. She loosened her tunic even more, unlacing the leather front, wishing for cooler climes. This desert didn't please her, not at all. She had been raised on a more temperate world and preferred those regions closer to the ice and snow than to desert.

Nothing about her apparel was suited for this heat. Her tunic chafed and rubbed her breasts, sweat pouring down the deep canyon between to tickle and torment. Her tight breeches made every step that much closer to agony. Even her boots, those fine fabrications from her home world done by her long-dead husband Reinhardt, seemed intent on making her miserable. Sand accumu-

lated inside, crunching and cutting into her feet. Heat
boiled upward through the thick soles and turned the
insides to ovens. And worst of all was the sword belt
suspended about her middle; she'd sooner die of heat
prostration than abandon her sword and belt, but it
weighted her down until she knew it had turned into
tons of inert steel instead of a single pound and a
half.

Inyx did not think of herself as a vain woman. She
scorned the courtiers of the cities intent only on fine
laces and silks and the most enticing of perfumes, but
she found herself wishing for just those things. A silk
tunic and breeches would be cooler. A lace scarf would
keep the sun off her neck while allowing sweat to
evaporate. And in place of a nice long, cool, bath to
ease the aches, remove the stench of travel and soothe
the body, Inyx prayed for even a small bottle of pungent perfume. Any odor, no matter how strong and
artificial, had to be better than that she emitted. How
long had it been since her last bath? The woman tried to
remember and failed.

"In this Iron Tongue I detect the man Claybore
would seek out. Tell me of him."

"Man? Iron Tongue? Hardly. He is a demon sent to
scourge our world. The empire of Bron and the city-
state of Wurrna are pledged to mutual destruction. And
of the evil lurking in Wurrna, Iron Tongue represents
the worst. I often think he flirts with insanity, sometimes deadly in his logic and rationality and other times
totally disconnected from his own tenuous humanity."

Inyx said nothing. Jacy warmed to his topic, building
a fine tirade against his enemy.

"He tortures small children. What he does to captured women is even worse, even more unspeakable. Of
the men he imprisons, we know but little. They are
forced into the power stone mines. None has ever
returned, none has escaped."

"How do you know Iron Tongue is so unspeakably evil, then?"

"He is!"

Inyx fell silent. She realized she touched on a matter of faith with the man. Societies built up careful myths to protect themselves from having to deal with too much reality. This perpetual battle between Bron and Wurnna smacked of such an origin.

"He speaks and all listen. It is impossible not to obey. The man is evil."

"Are you personally familiar with this?" Even as she asked, Inyx knew the answer.

"I am. In my younger, more foolish days, I crept into Wurnna thinking to free my brother, ten days lost in a raiding party. I entered the walls undetected, but luck ran with me. All the populace of that foul city had gathered to listen to that necromancer. He spoke and . . . the air rumbled. I cannot describe it. But the words were repugnant to me and I *believed*. I actually *believed* them. He spoke and evil became the pinnacle of goodness. He spoke and I wanted to help slay my very own brother."

"His name. How did Iron Tongue get his name?"

Noratumi shrugged. He obviously did not wish to pursue the topic further. The memory of his brother and his own abortive rescue wore too heavily on him.

"I would not speak of such things. Rather, let us talk of you. Tell me of your life. How did one so lovely come to be a traveler along the Road?"

Inyx began, her words hesitant at first but soon rolling forth with the man's encouragement. She found him a good listener, an attractive man, someone to unburden herself to now that Lan and Krek were gone. Even the heat became less of a bother as they walked and talked, sharing experiences and remembrances both pleasant and painful.

"When we arrive in Bron, there will be much rejoicing at such a discovery," said Noratumi.

"What discovery?"

"My discovery of a lady so beautiful, so charming. My discovery of *you*."

Somehow, she didn't see the need to object when his arm circled her waist and pulled her close.

Five days of heat and footweariness brought them to a valley filled with green growing plants and fragrant pine trees, a cool breeze blowing off crystal-clear streams fed by mountain snows, real dirt instead of sterile sand, and even occasional animals curiously studying them as they passed by burrow and nest.

"This is the southernmost part of my empire," Noratumi said proudly. "This is why we fight. To give up even one tiny lump of its soil is unthinkable."

"It is gorgeous," Inyx agreed, but some small part of her remained wary. For all the apparent tranquility about them, this was not a peaceful holding. She saw no signs of battle or armed troops, but wondered if the images, the shadows, of such remained as a stain on the land.

"Bron sits high atop a rocky spire. Gentle green meadows surround it and—" He was cut off by the return of his scout. The man ran up, out of breath. "Get decent, man," said Noratumi, reaching out and shaking the green-and-brown clad man by the shoulders. "Report."

"Sire, it is terrible!"

"What is, dammit? Don't go on like this."

"The grey-clads. They attack Bron!"

"So what else do you have to report? They were doing that when we left on our little sortie."

Inyx started to ask Noratumi the purpose of his mission into the desert, but he rushed on before she could properly frame the words. She had found that in this society questions had to be phrased in some fashion relating to the questioner's ranking, that of the interrogated, and some other criteria she had yet to discover. If the question went unheeded, it meant a mis-asking.

"All are within the city's walls, sire. You know what that means."

"Come, hurry, dammit. Don't dawdle. We must give what aid we can to our city."

"How can we be of assistance?" Inyx finally asked.

"When cut, they bleed like anyone else. My sword will drink deeply of their scurvy souls this day. I will not tolerate the grey soldiers meddling in my kingdom!"

Their advance slowed as they came to the main road through the valley-spanning empire. Under other circumstances, Inyx might have made a few rude comments about how ill-repaired the road was for such a mighty kingdom. She held all such criticism back, knowing that road repair ranked low on a list of priorities now. Even the smallest of kingdoms deserved better than Claybore's rule.

"There. See it, Inyx?" Jacy Noratumi pointed. Through the forest, rising above the treetops, surged the rocky pinnacle holding Bron. The stone walls of the city-state wavered as if they were still in the desert; the heated earth distorted sight. "Claybore's troops will be encamped in that direction, down in Kea Dell. Attacking the camp avails us nothing. We are too few for that to prove successful. But there are other things to do."

"You can't let them catch us between the main body of troops and their camp," protested Inyx. "There are too few of us to fight both toward and away from Bron."

Jacy Noratumi smiled wickedly.

"These are *my* forests. The grey interlopers know nothing of them. But come, I shall show you a small part of why they cannot take us as you suggest."

Noratumi gave hasty orders to his second in command, then drifted off as silent as any shadow into the forest. Inyx followed, matching his quiet. At first the man seemed surprised at her ability, then became occupied studying the soft brown loam.

"See? At least fifty mounted soldiers."

Inyx scanned the trees above, the boles and the ground before shaking her head.

"There were more. Notice the congestion of hoofprints here and here. Pieces of grey thread dangle from the bark, showing many rode off the path. Rains have caused some hardening of the earth at those points, but tracks have been left."

"Hmmm," mused Noratumi, "you are right. Very good." He looked at her with renewed admiration. "This path leads directly to Bron. And in that direction, the camp."

Falling silent, they moved on foot through the forests. After the desert, this was paradise for Inyx. She closed her eyes and inhaled deeply, taking in full odors rather than the abbreviated dryness she'd found on the sands. Here rose life, lush wetness, exciting breezes, real texture. And with it came the faint sounds of human voices.

Jacy unnecessarily motioned her to silence. On their bellies, they moved forward until they sighted the soldiers' camp.

Inyx had seen its ilk before. What worried her was the large number of mounts still tethered. If each one matched a soldier hidden away somewhere in the camp, there were a full hundred in reserve. To attack the other band would be stark foolishness on Noratumi's part if Claybore could summon up twice that number to take them from the rear.

Noratumi only smiled, then motioned Inyx away. They moved to the east, past a burbling stream and to a small waterfall.

Only under the cover of the rushing water did Jacy speak.

"Up there. Can you make it up on the rocks? They are slippery."

As agile as a mountain goat, Inyx leaped from rock to rock, found the tiniest of hand- and footholds, and scaled the rock face beside the waterfall with contemptuous ease. Noratumi found the going rougher; he was not only heavier, his boot toes were squared off and slipped on the precarious rock face.

Atop, waiting for Jacy, the woman studied the lake that created the waterfall. It stretched out for acres. But what attracted her attention was the cause of the waterfall. Some small aquatic creatures had built a dam across the river, restricting flow to the merest of trickles. The creatures allowed only enough flow over the top to reduce the pressure on their wood-and-mud structure.

"You begin to understand?" asked Noratumi, finally reaching the top. He stood beside Inyx on the lake shore and pointed to the elaborately constructed dam across the mouth of the lake. "That is our secret weapon."

"But how?"

He didn't answer. She realized the question had been improperly phrased and that the man's sense of propriety had been violated. Or perhaps he might have simply wanted to remain mysterious for her benefit. She cursed under her breath, wondering which it was. All the while Jacy worked, he spoke not a single word to her. Only slowly did Inyx come to understand the man's intent.

He lugged a huge fallen log down to the shoreline. Here, using vines, he lofted the log until it swung freely. He tied another vine to the log, then swam across to secure that end to a far tree. This caused the heavy tree trunk to hang suspended over the creatures' dam. If the vine on either side gave way, Inyx saw the destruction that would occur.

The heavy log would smash downward wrecking the dam; the water pressure would finish the destruction; the tiny stream escaping past the dam would become a torrential outpouring.

And the grey-clads' camp was on the stream—which would be turned into a raging river.

"But . . ." she began to ask again. She clamped her mouth firmly shut. Asking somehow insulted Noratumi. Let him show her, no matter how galled she got at having to wait.

The man vanished into the forest. Inyx sat on her haunches, idly twisting grasses into pulpy strands, discarding them and starting over. She did not have Lan's patience. Waiting annoyed her; she preferred immediate action to inactivity. But Jacy Noratumi finally returned. As silently as before, he scaled one tree and began smearing honey stolen from a hive onto the vine.

Inyx had to smile when she saw the dark arrow of a line of ants home in on the tasty treat. They went directly up the tree, across the limb, down the vine and began eating the honey, even before Noratumi had finished.

He dropped to the ground and washed his hands in the lake. Only then did he speak.

"Past experience tells me we have only an hour before the hungry beggars chew through enough of the vine to bring down the log. Let us hurry to the attack! We have a battle to win this day!"

They hastened to rejoin Noratumi's small band, now stripped of their travel gear and arrayed in full battle dress. The horses nervously shuffled and pawed at the earth, aware of the impending fight.

"How much longer before the dam breaks?" Inyx asked, as she slipped into what had been Margora's padded armor. She started to ask again when she realized that Jacy was ignoring her; the question of their relative rankings had yet to be resolved. Inyx pushed down her irritation at being left in this social limbo. Noratumi enjoyed her company and even sought it out on their trek back to Bron, but she had the feeling of being treated as a diversion rather than a human at times.

And at other times, he had made her think she was nothing less than a princess. Inyx had been among many peoples with different customs. Leaning the ways of Bron required time. When she did figure out what the rules were, Noratumi's behavior wouldn't seem as odd. She might not approve of it then, but understanding would be hers.

"To the city!" the man called from the front of the pathetic column. Inyx admired his determination, but to attack with such a small group against fully fifty armed and ready soldiers smacked of insanity. However, it was an insanity she could share. Pulling free her sword, she thrust it upward as if to gut the sky. The sun caught the blued steel and sent shafts of brilliance radiating toward Bron.

Noratumi used this as a signal for the attack. Pell mell they thundered toward the meadow road leading to the front gate of the city. Shouting until she was hoarse, Inyx entered the green meadow—and the battle.

Immediately came five riders. Something singled her out from the others. She had no time to decide what this might have been. The five attacked. And she charged.

Between them she raced, her horse straining to the utmost. Her blade flashed first left and then right, leaving behind lacerated wrists and cursing riders. She ducked under a heavy battle axe, leaned forward, and stabbed with her sword at the axe-wielder, and was rewarded by a liquid cry of anguish as her blade penetrated the exposed area under the man's arm. He snorted blood from his nostrils, a sure sign she had punctured not only skin but lung. The man toppled off his horse, sending the animal racing off in confusion.

"Jacy! Do you need help?" she cried, laughing even as she parried a spear-lunge. Jacy Noratumi turned, stared at her with emotionless amber eyes, and shook his head. It was all the answer she expected. Then Inyx found herself engaged with two riders, one of whom carried red officer's stripes on a sleeve.

Like Lan Martak, she had never been able to decipher the ranking system used by the grey-clads, but the red stripes indicated more than a simple soldier. A deft twist of her wrist disengaged her blade and sent it snaking into the other man's throat. She faced the leader of Claybore's troops.

They hacked and hammered at one another until Inyx's arm turned to lead. Knowing that she could not fight in this fashion much longer, Inyx changed tactics. Allowing her sword to be knocked aside, she made no effort to return to line. Instead, she rose up in her stirrups and hurled herself onto her opponent. Both tumbled to the ground in a kicking, swearing pile.

The officer rolled free and came to her feet. She tossed back her helm, allowing a flow of medium-length blonde hair to catch the wind. A sneer marked her already-scarred face.

"So you are the or. Claybore seeks," she said, the sibilance of her voice so great she hissed like a snake. "Promotion shall be mine when I deliver you to our leader."

Inyx laughed harshly, reaching to her belt and pulling forth her dagger.

"It'll take more than words, bitch."

Inyx tried to stop the woman from making a quick signal to another grey-clad at the edge of the meadow; then she had to smile. That signal could mean only one thing: the reserves had been summoned from the camp. It was only a matter of moments before Noratumi's carefully wrought trap was sprung, bringing watery death to all downhill.

"Laugh if you will," came the words laden with scorn. "Claybore will place your head on a pike outside his palace. I will be made ruler of this entire planet."

"Not if he doesn't regain his tongue," said Inyx.

The expression on the other woman's face was worth the effort. The surprise momentarily froze her opponent; Inyx lunged forward, dagger tip leading the way. She pinked the officer's left arm. Not a serious wound, but enough to produce a slowing. Then would come death.

"You know nothing!" shrieked Claybore's commander. She rushed forward, batted Inyx's knife out of the way, and locked arms around the woman's back, pinning her arms to her side. Inyx grunted as the woman applied pressure to the bear hug. Kick as she might, Inyx found herself unable to break free. Bending backwards, her breath gusting from her lungs, Inyx felt her spine cracking and her consciousness fleeing.

Again surprise came to her rescue. A loud roaring followed by anguished cries of death echoed up from the forests. For the barest instant, Claybore's commander hesitated. Inyx butted her head directly into the nose. She felt a gush of warm red coppery-smelling blood as cartilage broke. The woman screamed in pain and rage and Inyx kicked free.

The officer held her broken nose as she looked from Inyx to the torrential outpourings raging through the forest. She watched her reserves washed away, their armor too heavy for easy escape. That very armor protecting from sword and arrow now weighed them down to a watery death.

"It's not as easy as you thought, is it?"

"Slut!" screamed the officer.

Rage worked against her. She lost her ability to think; Inyx sidestepped quickly and plunged her dagger deep into her opponent's groin, the tip finding the nerve center in the hypogastrium. The blonde gasped, stiffened, then fell forward as if a woodsman's axe had felled the largest tree in the forest. Panting, covered with blood—from her opponents—Inyx stepped back and surveyed the course of the battle.

To her astonishment, Noratumi had not underestimated the fighting prowess of his tiny band. They had met and defeated Claybore's larger company.

"Not a bad day's work," crowed Jacy Noratumi, riding up. "Most were killed here in the meadow, totally routed down in the forest. It'll be a week before the dam is in place again, but that's small loss. Come, join me." A brawny arm reached down for Inyx to take. She twisted up behind Noratumi, who spurred toward the gates leading into Bron.

"Your people fight well. I'd thought this would be suicidal."

"You fight magnificently yourself. The feast this evening in your honor will be. . . ." Noratumi's words trailed off as the survivors reformed into a single-file line.

Inyx leaned around the man and stared up the road. The shimmering she had noted from a distance grew worse. The stone walls protecting Bron rippled and danced like reflections in a pond. A thin line of dust on the road held her attention. Not only was the dust pulled up into tiny whirlwinds, the motes trapped in the cones of wind sparkled with a deadly inner light.

"Jacy, don't," she said, but he had already seen the danger.

The lead rider had been too eager to return home. Whipping his horse to a gallop, he had ridden full into that barely visible barrier—and had *flashed* out of existence. Not bone, not hair, nothing remained to show he or his mount had ever existed.

They had defeated Claybore's troops. To enter Bron they had to now defeat his magics.

CHAPTER FOUR

Dancing in front of him came a six-armed horror. Each arm ended in tiny tendrils clutching swords, axes, and flails designed to rip the flesh from his bones. Lan Martak croaked out a warning to Krek, clumsily drew his sword, and prepared to fight.

The creature rushed forth—and through him.

Lan blinked, then sank to his knees, supporting himself on his sword. He didn't look behind to follow the path taken by the apparition. He knew now it had been a mirage, a product of his own feverish imagination—or of Claybore's.

"Friend Lan Martak, why do you stop to rest like that? Your knees will burn in this awful heat. Why, my own claws are beginning to melt from the heat. Imagine, chiton melting. It is terrible the hardships I must endure. The degradation of it all! How am I to get about if I have to hobble like some human, only using two legs. Two legs! The disgrace of it is unimaginable to you, I am sure."

"I'm all right, Krek. It . . . it's nothing."

The spider turned his head around in a circle that would have been impossible for a human to mimic and said gently, "Claybore sends his visions again?"

"Possibly. Or I might be hallucinating. I haven't had enough water. The magics to condense the water take too much out of me now, even if it is a simple spell. And the heat. Damn this heat!"

"On this point, we are in complete agreement. Let us not dally here. I can almost feel the coolness of mountain winds rustling through my furry legs."

The young warrior heaved himself to his feet and closed weary eyes, reaching deep within himself for strength. He knew magical spells that enhanced physical power, but he shied away from chanting them. The higher he pushed himself with such spells, the more time it took to recover. The energy use had to be reserved for those times when instant strength was needed. He would be dead within the hour if now he tried to push his endurance magically.

That did not prevent him from using other spells, others requiring only tiny portions of his energy. He reached out and found a tiny glowing spark, fanned it alive magically, allowed it to grow and glow and spin and dazzle his inner eye.

He cast it forth.

It appeared to speed off, diminish with distance, circle the entire universe and then return, all within the span of a rapid heartbeat. He examined the information brought back to him by the mote of light. He sighed when it verified what he had feared.

Claybore's power grew moment by moment. The sorcerer expended more time and spells against him in an effort to prevent Lan and Krek from reaching the relative safety of the mountains. The desert aided Lan. To attack magically over long distances sapped even Claybore's augmented power.

Lan wondered at how potent Claybore would be if he regained all his body's segments. Even as the thought crossed his mind, he pushed it away. Claybore was considerably stronger than Lan with just heart, head, and torso. Another addition to his severed body would put him beyond Lan's reach.

The young mage examined the dancing mote of energy once more before freeing it to return into other dimensions. All the information possible had been milked from it.

"Claybore cannot attack us directly," he told his spider friend. "He is occupied in some other battle. I had glimpses of another mage, a potent one. The name Iron Tongue intruded repeatedly."

"Is it possible this Iron Tongue actually has within his head Claybore's tongue?"

Lan shrugged.

"Whoever he is or whatever power he possesses, he and Claybore are locked in a death fight. I also sensed that Claybore's attention is divided in another direction."

"Inyx?"

"I fear so. It might be best to draw his attention away by some magical attack."

"Can you do it? Your voice comes out weak and broken. Almost as weak and broken as I feel. Oh woe! Why do I walk the Road? I shall die, I know I will die in this web-forsaken, desolate place."

Lan kept his eyes closed. His lips moved in a cracked cadence as he employed his energy-giving spell, but he directed it not at himself but at Krek. In direct proportion, he felt himself increasingly drained as the spider perked up. When Krek bounded to his feet, almost as agile as his healthy self, Lan stopped the chant. A few seconds more and Lan himself would have been unable to walk.

"I do feel ever so much better after this brief respite. Do come along, friend Lan Martak. It is only a short jaunt to the mountains. Not far at all."

Krek bounced off, his uneven gait faster than Lan could match. The human didn't care. He might move slower now that he had transferred some of his energy to Krek, but that didn't mean he wouldn't arrive sooner or later. Lan Martak had learned much of his own limits since walking the Road. He plunged to new depths of exhaustion only because his burgeoning magical powers gave him new heights of energy.

"Move," he mumbled to himself. "One foot, then the other. Move, move, move!"

All day he maintained this ritual. Twilight descended and cooler winds blew into his face. He hardly noticed. He kept up his snail's pace. The only change that penetrated was under his feet. Crusted sand dunes became tiny pebbles, which changed into solid rock. By the time he heard Krek's damnably cheerful voice, he struggled along an arroyo dotted with increasingly lush vegetation.

"We're out of the desert," he heard himself saying, almost in disbelief. "We made it!"

"Of course we made it, you silly human. I never doubted for a moment we would. Here, look. See? Is this not the most wonderful pond you have ever seen?"

"What? Pond? Water!"

"Oh, yes, it is that. I referred to the waterbugs. So tasty. Succulent, even."

The arachnid bobbed up and down, mandibles dextrously snapping closed on one insect after another. Krek became so greedy he had to use two of his front legs to force the bugs into his mouth. Lan paid him no attention. Falling flat on his stomach, he plunged his head under the cool, fresh surface of the tiny pond. Only when he began to gasp for air did he surface, sputtering and letting the restoring water run down his face.

"Are you going to drink that terrible fluid or simply play in it?" demanded Krek. "It appalls me watching you frolic and cavort about so. In water. How absolutely disgusting." The spider quivered all over to make his point.

"A year's rest wouldn't do me more good at the

moment," Lan said, hardly exaggerating. This time
when he plunged his face down to the rippling surface,
he drank. Slowly at first, then with greater need. He
forced himself to stop. His body required a certain
length of time before it absorbed what he had drunk. A
few minutes later, he again sampled the water. Whatever happened, he didn't want to take in too much and
make himself sick.

Lounging back, bare feet in the water and the shadow
of a large rock protecting him from the sun, Lan vented
a deep, heartfelt sigh.

"It's been hard, old spider, but the going gets easier
from here on."

"How is that?" Krek appeared distracted. He canted
his head to one side, as if listening to faint sounds in
the distance.

Lan concentrated and heard nothing. He'd never been
clear on whether or not Krek's hearing was more acute
than his own. The spider's senses were definitely not
those of a human. The large saucer-sized dun eyes
lacked the segmenting of smaller arachnids, but those
deep eyes were by no means human-appearing. Krek
claimed to have no sense of smell and Lan believed
what "taste" the spider displayed relied more on the
succulence than the flavor of what he devoured. The
juicier the bug, the more he enjoyed it. One sense that
Krek possessed that far outstripped Lan's was that of
feel. Digging down into the earth, Krek could detect the
faintest of vibrations long before his human companion
received any hint of movement.

"Do you feel something moving about?" he asked.

"No." The answer came curt and uncharacteristi-
cally short.

Lan closed his eyes and forced his tiny mote of light
into existence again. He sent it forth, but it returned
quickly and without new information. Using it too often
might be dangerous, he knew. Claybore's magics were

more sophisticated; the light mote might lead the older sorcerer back to his adversary. Also, Lan Martak knew little of the magics powering the mote. Discovering it by accident, he had simply used it. What it was, where it came from, and why it even existed were questions he had not tried to answer. Simply surviving Claybore's magical onslaughts was too engrossing for him to do much experimenting.

"Tell me what it is, Krek."

"I sense . . . something. I hardly dare believe I can be so lucky."

"Lucky?"

"There are . . . others near." Again the vagueness irritated Lan, but he pushed it from his mind. Let his friend be mysterious for a while. His magical senses told him they were relatively safe. He needed to rest. The battles in the Twistings, the chase across worlds, the encounter with Alberto Silvain at the oasis, and then the deadly trek to these mountains had sapped his reserves.

He fell into a deep sleep.

And Claybore visited him with even more frightening nightmares. He slept, but he did not rest.

"They will be at this city-state of Bron soon," said Krek. "Do you not wish to hurry after Inyx?"

"I'm recovering," Lan told the spider. "My energy levels feel about up to normal. Maybe even more than normal." The surges and pulses of magic he controlled surpassed anything he had dealt with before. Lan Martak knew he still lacked the skills to confront Claybore directly, but he also knew he had sufficient strength now to pursue the worlds-spanning battle.

"Inyx awaits you."

The spider's insistence troubled Lan. He didn't want to appear too eager to chase after Inyx—and Jacy Noratumi—but it continually rose to his mind that he did not like her being with the man. Jealousy? That was as handy a word as any for what he felt. No matter how he tried, he couldn't push it aside.

"Very well. Let's keep well into the mountains where there's water and bugs and start for Bron."

He rose and started off in the proper direction. Krek didn't move.

"Come on. You were the one demanding we get a-hiking."

"Not that way. There is a valley down there."

"So?" Lan used a minor spell to check for other magic use. He found no indication of humans, much less magical spells waiting to trip him up. Only faint magical emanations came from a distance, and these he discounted as meaningless.

"Spiders. Others. Like me."

The young warrior-mage frowned. Whenever Krek became reticent, he was holding back important information. The normally loquacious spider had been abnormally quiet the past days while they rested for their journey to Bron.

"Is that a danger?"

"You passed only briefly through the Egrii Mountains and did not encounter others of my kind."

"I met your bride Klawn." Lan swallowed hard at the thought. Krek was several feet taller than the human, and Lan counted as tall. Klawn dwarfed Krek in all ways, including her singlemindedness.

"She is such a petite thing, is she not?" The arachnid sighed happily. "I do so wish she might be here."

"The others, Krek, the others."

"What? Oh, yes. Those even in my web had little use for humans. Always disturbing us with your rumbling wagons, those hideous demon-powered engines coughing and whining, never stopping for a pleasant chat, always assuming you were masters of the high reaches. Most of my clan enjoyed eating humans."

Krek's mandibles clacked shut in an unconscious gesture.

Lan only winced.

"We tried to reason with you humans, but it bought us little enough. So we tried charging for every caravan that used our passes. Some of you even tried sneaking through. You can imagine how that distressed us." Again the clack of razor-sharp mandibles.

"That's how you accumulated your web treasure. The, uh, tariffs on humans."

"Exactly. But few of my kind ever *liked* humans, even when you paid the paltry fees due us. And truth to tell, you are not very good food."

"You're trying to tell me these mountain arachnids might like humans even less."

"That puts it succinctly enough. Of course, they will welcome me. I am a visiting Webmaster. We spiders arrange the proper protocol, always. As long as it is clear I have no intention of remaining in the area for very long, the local Webmaster will greet me like a long-lost cousin. Which I am."

Lan considered what he remembered of the lay of the land. The valley ahead provided the quickest route to Bron, a distance not more than two days' travel. Krek's not too subtle hints had lit the fires of anguish inside him; he must hasten to rejoin Inyx to put them to rest. But skirting the valley and finding another road through the mountains might cost precious days—or even weeks.

"I'm sure you can convince them that I, too, am just passing through and pose no threat to them. I might even be able to gift them in some way, using a few of my spells."

"Such as your fire spell?" Krek's voice almost broke from the loathing. The only thing he hated worse than water was fire. His tinder-dry leg fur would turn him into a blazing bonfire if he became too careless.

"I had other things in mind. A hunting spell might

please them. I could roust out all the insects in the valley and trot them down for your friends.''

"They might not be my friends."

"Your fellow spiders," Lan corrected. "I'm sure such a trade—the bugs for safe passage—would be satisfactory for all parties."

Krek hesitated, then bobbed his head in agreement. Lan couldn't tell how enthusiastic the spider was about the idea, but it hardly mattered. Lan felt the pressure of time mouting on him again, and not just to rejoin his beloved. Claybore fought on two fronts. If one should turn into a victory for the mage, he might spend more time seeking out Lan.

"Let's be off."

Krek didn't answer.

A full day of hiking brought them to the lip of a valley as lush and pretty as any Lan Martak had ever seen. The tiny stream meandering down the center caused huge trees to thrust skyward. From these limbs soared spider webs as thick as his wrist. Fastened on valley walls, trees, rock spires, each other, those webs criss-crossed the entire air above the floor. Caught in the webs were birds of prey as large as the dire-eagles that inhabited the el-Liot Mountains on Lan's home world. He thanked all the powers of the universe that he need not rely on wing power to get through the canyon.

"Down?" asked Krek.

"Of course. Polish up on your spider talk. I see a delegation coming now." The human pointed at three tiny black dots that grew with amazing rapidity until they took on detail as full-sized arachnids rivaling Krek in bulk.

"Stay here," ordered the spider. He ambled forward and planted himself a few yards away. While his friend waited, Lan studied the webs more carefully. Some strands were sticky while others—the aerial walkways for the spiders—were simply ropelike. The intricate geometric patterns appeared to be the individual spinner's signature, just as a human painter signed his oils. When Lan's eyes tired of tracing the spirals and twists, he focused once more on his friend.

Krek spoke with great animation to two of the three. The third spider remained high above in his web, a sentry to guard against treachery. Lan understood none of the rapid talk but guessed that it went well. Krek was relaxed and the object of some deference. His theory of being greeted as a wandering Webmaster turned into fact.

"How goes it?" Lan asked, his voice pitched to carry downslope to where Krek and the others hunkered down and talked.

In a deceptively mild, unhurried response, Krek called back, "I advise you to run for your life, friend Lan Martak. These are honorable friends—of mine. Toward you they show nothing but animosity. I do believe they wish to eat you, even though I have warned them you carry a foul taste."

"What?"

"I do not jest. Run for your life. I shall try to dissuade them, but even my talents in this arena might prove too small."

The youth hesitated, not sure if Krek made fun of him or not. A quick look overhead convinced him of his danger. The sentry spider had spun a walking web between his perch and a rock to Lan's right. The arachnid balanced on the thick strand and came straight for the human. The intent was all too clear.

Lan's mind raced. A fire spell would burn the web out from under the spider. It might also set fire to other webs. A conflagration raging through the valley might kill many of the spiders trapped on their webs. While he had no desire to murder them, he had even less desire to be killed by them.

Behind was the terrain they had covered since enter-

ing the mountains. He might return to the spring they'd
first encountered and from there reenter the desert and
follow Inyx to Bron. Or he might push on, hope that
Krek could stay them long enough, and reach the far
side of the valley and be days closer to Bron.

His decision made, Lan Martak ran forward, dodging
past Krek and the others and down into the valley. He
sprinted hard, enjoying the feel of his muscles so
smoothly responding. When he entered the worlds of
magic, he had scant use for muscle. The power of the
mind was all. But he had grown up in forests, living
by his wits and strong arm, enjoying rare-cooked haunch
of deer and other game.

He smiled in relief when he saw no pursuit formed
behind. Both spiders continued to talk with Krek and
the guard above remained high on the rim of the valley
and did not drop down to chase him.

Lan fell into a ground-devouring pace that allowed
him to move with fluid, effortless grace. Around him
the tranquility of the forests supplied him with new
power, new stamina. Occasionally a shadow of an overhead spider web crossed his path, but these were rare.
When he reached the far side, he'd wait for Krek to
catch up.

Would he gloat then! Krek always chided him for
being so slow, for not having the proper number of legs
to adequately propel him. For once he'd beat Krek.

The sounds of the forest died suddenly. Lan ran a
few paces, then stopped, listening hard for the cause of
this disturbing inactivity. He heard nothing. Frowning,
he scanned the trees and underbrush hoping for a sign
of what was wrong. Nothing.

Then he remembered to look above.

The sky blackened with the massive bodies of a
thousand spiders. They swung from web to web until
they congregated above him, blocking out the sun. It
was as if night had fallen in midday.

"No," he whispered, holding back the spells that would send gouts of flame leaping upward. Wanton killing would solve nothing; he realized the futility of attempting to slay so many opponents.

Frantically looking around, he saw a tiny stream wetly thrusting itself out from a rocky face in the canyon wall, a minor tributary feeding the larger creek in the middle of the valley. He sprinted for it, hoping the spiders would stay away from the water. On their aerial highway, they were not in the least inconvenienced. Heavy strands spatted onto the rock face beside him. Spiders began sliding downward toward him, intent on their pursuit.

Lan jerked free his sword and slashed at the strand nearest him. His blade cleanly sliced through, sending the spider tumbling to the valley floor behind. He eliminated another and another of the strands in this fashion until it occurred to him that he only signed his own death warrant.

There was no way he could cut all the strands. For every one he hacked, two more were firmly secured to the rock wall just beyond his reach. In minutes, he would be surrounded by spiders.

He had seen Krek's mandibles break a steel sword.

The stream burbled mindlessly as it made its way to the valley floor. Lan looked up, into the reaches from whence it sprang. A tiny opening, hardly large enough for his muscular body, gave him a small chance for escape. He clumsily worked up a narrow chimney with the water flowing between his legs, found the opening, and began wiggling through.

For a moment, his bulk plugged the stream. He sputtered as the dammed water rose above his head. Jerking about, skinning his shoulders, he forced his way through and into a small pool behind the hole. Released water roared around him, then returned to a quieter flow.

The man stared back through the small hole; a huge brown eye glared back.

"Aieee!" he started, then calmed. The following spider was too large to fit through the hole, even if the water threat was to be endured. But Lan realized his escape was going to be of short duration. He knew Krek could work up and down mountains with little effort. Scaling the cliffs overlooking the valley would be simplicity itself for these spiders. In no time they'd be above him again.

Lan Martak splashed loudly through the pool, up onto a sandy embankment and then ran as though all the demons of the Lower Places nipped at his heels. He lost track of the turnings made by the stream, but the journey was continually uphill. When the stream vanished totally, the young mage stopped to study it. An artesian spring thrust upward from the rock and fed the tiny river.

Glancing around, he saw he had emerged from the valley and stood on a rocky ridge. To his right stretched the distance-hazy green of the valley of spiders. Ahead lay even more treacherous mountain terrain. To the left—and far, far down—raged a river.

"It's either ahead or back," he said to himself. Ahead didn't promise anything but sore feet and hard work. He turned to head back in the direction where he and Krek had originally entered the mountainous region and gasped.

Not one, but fully a hundred spiders advanced on him.

Again he fought to restrain himself. A fire spell would fry them in their tracks. But there might be another way out. There had to be. Wanton killing accomplished nothing.

The river so far below beckoned. A pathway down the rock face might exist. He ran to the edge and stared down into a five-hundred-foot drop. The sheer granite face put the lie to any such escape existing. Climbing down would require mountaineering gear—and time he didn't have.

"I hope the river's deep," he said, taking a breath. The spiders advanced, mandibles slashing at the air. Lan Martak took two running steps and leaped out into space. And fell and fell and fell.

CHAPTER FIVE

Metallic clanking and the subliminal hum of magics filled the air. Alberto Silvain pushed back from the table and stood at attention as Claybore entered the room.

"Master!" the man cried, bringing his clenched fist to his heart in salute.

Claybore did not answer—at least with human lips. The words swelled and flowed, filling Silvain's ears and mind, but no physical sound came from the fleshless skull poised atop the armless torso. This grisly pairing was supported by a mechanical body of steel wire and wheels, long metal shins and arms, and a magic spell that caused it to glow a pale blue as it moved.

Empty eye sockets in the skull boiled with darkness, then flared forth brilliant crimson beams. Silvain stood absolutely still as the twin beams blasted through the space on either side of his arms. He felt the heat, the stinging, searing destructiveness so near and did not flinch. To have done so would have meant death.

The mechanical turned about, and the death beams vanished. Silvain slumped slightly. Claybore was angry with him for the debacle in the Twistings, but not so wroth that he would kill.

The mech struck a pose, spindly arms on nonexistent hips. The torso appeared human enough, but a pearly light shone forth from the region of the heart. Silvain knew no heart beat within the breast; the Kinetic Sphere pulsed there. That globe allowed Claybore to slip from world to world without using the cenotaphs. In conquest of that particular organ, he had thought himself ultimately triumphant, but that fool Martak and the others had proven otherwise.

"You failed," came the words ringing inside Silvain's head.

"I offer no excuse."

"Good. None is expected—or accepted."

"I will not fail again."

"Failure a second time means death. I have been lenient with you because of past victories. Silvain, I cannot tolerate another failure. I *must* triumph on this world."

"While I have been here only a short time, I have examined the assembled documents. Conquest goes well."

"Fool!" raged Claybore, the swirlings of ruby light forming in the eye sockets of his skull once more. "Who cares for mere territory? I fight a battle spanning entire worlds! I must find those parts of me Terrill scattered along the Road. *That* is my goal, not some mudball spinning stupidly through space."

"I err."

"Where is k'Adesina?"

"Here, Lord."

Alberto Silvain turned to see a small, almost fragile woman enter the room. She held herself proudly erect, her brown hair cut short to form a skullcap. What she lacked in stature she more than made up for in intensity. Silvain blinked as he looked at her. More than ambition drove her—but what could that something else be?

"You two have much in common," said Claybore. "You have both failed me."

"The spider's webbing prevented me from slaying Lan Martak for you, Lord. It will not happen—"

"Silence!" roared Claybore. "Excuses. You both make the same excuses and the same promises. 'It won't happen again,' " he mocked. "No, it won't. You will succeed this time. Both of you."

Silvain frowned, wondering what this k'Adesina woman had done. It would take a while to build a new intelligence network among the grey-clad soldiers populating this world, but it would be worth the effort. He needed information if he wanted to serve Claybore. Data on this woman ranked highly on his list of items to learn. She carried rank equal to his own.

"Report, Kiska," the mage commanded. The mechanical clanked as it shifted position. Silvain felt uneasiness at the movement; the skull's eye sockets stared blankly at him.

The woman cleared her throat and began. "Since coming to this world through the cenotaph atop Mount Tartanius, I have organized four major offensives."

"Get on with it," snapped Claybore. "I need to know the precise problems we face as of this instant."

"Very well, Lord. Subjugation is complete except for three areas." Silvain perked up, listening intently. The woman's voice took on added timbre. She became totally enmeshed in the telling.

"The valley of spiders, Bron, and Wurnna," supplied Claybore. "The spiders are insignificant. They have nothing that interests me. Is what I seek in Bron or Wurnna?"

"The city-state of Bron is under seige. While our troops have suffered unexplained losses recently, the city itself is permanently sealed by spells. No one enters or leaves."

"But I still *feel* my tongue!"

"Yes, Lord," the woman went on, excitement entering her voice. "Your tongue is in Wurnna."

"Damn!"

"The sorcerers of that city easily counter our mages' best spells. They repulse our most fervent attacks. It is my belief that their leader, known as Iron Tongue, either has in his immediate possession, or knows the whereabouts of, your tongue."

"With a name like that, he must employ the tongue on a regular basis," supplied Silvain. He drummed nervous fingers on the tabletop in front of him. "Is it possible he carries the tongue inside his mouth—in place of his own natural tongue?"

"It is possible," said Claybore.

"Directing further efforts toward Bron seems wasteful. I suggest all attention be focused on Wurnna and the sorcerers within it. For that, Lord, we need your aid."

"It shall be available. But I would like the two of you to work out a strategy for physical conquest. At the precise moment I launch my sorcerous assault, I want all within Wurnna to fear for their mortal bodies. Have such a plan prepared for my examination no later than midnight."

Both Silvain and k'Adesina snapped to rigid attention as the mechanical carrying Claybore's torso and skull glowed a deeper blue and walked swiftly from the room. Albert Silvain sank to his chair in relief when the mech had vanished.

"What did you do wrong?" he asked k'Adesina.

Her chocolate eyes blazed.

"My defeat was small compared to yours. I did not lose our lord a bodily part. I merely failed to destroy Martak and the spider." She sneered as she added, "Even without Claybore's urging, I would gladly slay Martak."

"Why?" Silvain heard the personal animosity toward the young warrior ringing out like a black bell.

"He killed my husband."

"Martak has led a checkered past, it seems. And one more impressive than I had thought."

"I had him in my grasp and I lost him," Kiska k'Adesina said, her words quavering with emotion. "That will not happen again. This time he will be mine!"

"I rather think our duties lie in obtaining for our lord what he seeks," Silvain said dryly. He brushed away imaginary wrinkles in the map before them and looked it over. The stone hut they huddled in was centrally located to both Bron and the city of sorcerers. Claybore's entire encampment could be shifted to either target quickly; earlier subjugation had gone well and left the two most difficult goals close to one another, allowing concentration of forces. Silvain stroked the stubble on his chin, ran his finger over the rough parchment map, then indicated a star on the chart, asking, "This is the location of Wurnna?"

A curt nod.

"So. I believe a frontal assault in such a fashion gives the greatest chance for success." He sketched out the paths for k'Adesina.

"No," she said emphatically. "This is not the way."

"May one inquire why not?" Silvain's pride had been injured by her adamant denial. He fancied himself a master tactician and was unused to having anyone contradict him. While he had failed in the Twistings, it had been due to unforeseen powers controlled by Lan Martak and not from any lack of genius on his part.

"This canyon—this corridor leading to the gates of Wurnna—is off limits for our troops. A man standing on the battlements can whisper and be heard throughout the canyon."

"So?" Then understanding burst upon Silvain. "The tongue. This Iron Tongue can turn our soldiers against us. Is this organ so potent?"

"It is. What once belonged to Claybore produces magics of the first water when used by another. Iron Tongue speaks; all who hear him believe without question."

"Can Claybore conjure against its use?"

"That is the tongue's power. It enhances spells tenfold. Perhaps a thousandfold. I am no sorcerer and cannot say for sure. This I do know. As long as Iron Tongue uses it, we must beware of sending troops to their death."

Silvain laughed harshly. "Let them die. What we must guard against is this Iron Tongue turning them against us." He saw that Kiska k'Adesina agreed. He went on, warming to the topic. "Let us think on possible approaches and meet once again in, say, one hour."

"That sounds logical. That will still give us a few hours before midnight to work out a plan together." Her brown eyes locked on his cold dark ones.

"Yes," Silvain said slowly. "Together. Definitely together."

He folded the map and left the room, his thoughts on more than battle tactics.

"Should we take the time to torture him?" Alberto Silvain asked. The woman's expression told him the answer. She wanted to see pain inflicted and would not be swayed, no matter how pressing other matters became. Silvain idly wondered if k'Adesina would risk Claybore's displeasure over this.

"There are new magics my torturer wishes to show us," the brown-haired woman replied tartly. "I would see them."

"Very well." An indolent wave of the hand hid Silvain's real interest. He had never considered magic a fit instrument for torture. Such inventiveness added new dimensions to Kiska k'Adesina's convoluted character.

She snapped her fingers, then reclined in the high-backed carved wood chair dominating the simple stone hut. Numerous others before her in the chair had left stains and burns on the broad arms. Her own fingers threatened to put in new depressions. Silvain smiled slightly at her tension. It was the eagerness of a horse in a race that affected her, not fear. She *yearned* for this torture.

"Milord, milady," said the effeminate man at the side of the room. "With your kind permission I shall begin."

K'Adesina nodded curtly. The mage-torturer's expression never changed as he began muttering a chant under his breath. Silvain strained to catch the words. The rhythm seemed oddly familiar, but the words eluded him. All chance of overhearing and learning a precious new spell fled when a shriek of pure agony filled the chamber.

"There," said Kiska k'Adesina. "One of the men captured at the debacle in front of Bron. I ordered him brought here to discover the true nature of that fiasco."

Silvain tented fingers and balanced his chin on the ridge formed by the tips. He dispassionately studied the poor wight being dragged into the chamber on barbs of pure magic.

Fight as he would, the prisoner couldn't escape a tiny yellow circle on the dirt floor. Hands pressed against unseen barriers. But there was no exit except death; the man failed to appreciate that. Silvain immediately pegged the man as a lowly soldier, probably nothing more than a spear-carrier.

"Can you learn anything from the likes of him?" he asked k'Adesina.

"We shall see. My Patriccan is most skilled."

Silvain only shrugged. His attentions turned from the prisoner's cries for mercy that would never come to Kiska k'Adesina. Her rapt gaze told him she obtained more than information. To her this was a sexual stimulus, an aphrodisiac. Or was it a mere substitute? That was an item to be explored later.

"How did Noratumi destroy a full company of our soldiers?" she demanded.

"Lady, release me. I . . . I will tell alllll!" The plea fell on deaf ears. She motioned to Patriccan. The old, wizened mage rubbed gnarled hands together and began repeating the chant Silvain had noted earlier.

The yellow circle on which the prisoner stood began to turn from yellow to a deep gold, then it became orange and red and red-white and finally white-hot. The captive danced like a bug on a griddle, unable to leave the ring of magic and slowly charring from the soles of his feet upward.

"What spell did Noratumi use to defeat our troops?" she asked again, her voice rising in pitch.

"He . . . he is no sorcerer. He hates them. We of Bron war against Wurnna."

"That much seems apparent," said Silvain. "These reports verify it." He tapped his knuckles against a closed leather-bound book on the table in front of him. Leaning back, he hiked feet to the tabletop, watching both the victim and k'Adesina past his boots. Silvain presented the perfect picture of a feline at rest.

"Up," the woman ordered her mage. Patriccan's hands rose slightly, witchlight glowing at his wrinkled fingertips. The effect on the prisoner was even more startling. The white-hot circle began to lift from the dirt floor. When it reached the man's knees, his cries became totally incoherent.

"How can you get decent information when he babbles like that?" asked Silvain. "You, Patriccan. Clarify his words."

"A mind burn, Lord?"

"That might be interesting."

"*I* am conducting this, Silvain," the woman snapped. "I decide what is to be done to this fool."

"It is only a suggestion. I have never used magics in this fashion before, but a mind burn proves most effective during battle, when the opposing leader can be singled out."

"Do it," Kiska k'Adesina said with ill-concealed anger. Silvain lounged back, content now to watch. Agitating the woman further served no purpose. He had learned as much about her as he desired. For the moment. It was the mage that drew his attention now. The spells used were variants of simple fire-starting chants, but with certain arcane twists. While no mage himself, Silvain maintained an arsenal of certain useful spells. The time might come when one served him well.

The white ring of fire rose quickly past the prisoner's knees, waist, chest, neck. It stopped short of his chin. Like a man drowning, he fought to keep his face above the blazing circle threatening to destroy him. Tears of pain ran down the man's face and sizzled hotly on the magical ring.

"The mind burn," Patriccan announced in a low voice. Both hands and words combined now, a wringing motion coordinated with the cadence of his chant. The victim stiffened, all trace of pain gone.

"This strips away layer after layer of memory until nothing is left. I liken it to sunburned skin peeling away."

"Don't lecture, Patriccan. Just do it."

K'Adesina waited while the prisoner began to babble. Skillfully, the ancient mage only allowed those words to escape that pertained to Kiska k'Adesina's question. The story of how Noratumi had arranged for the log to smash the dam and flood the grey-clads' camp poured out, just as the trapped waters had. Then nothing more left the prisoner's mouth.

"His brain is gone, milady. Burned away like mist in the morning sun."

"How poetic. Do with him what you will."

For the first time, Patriccan smiled. Silvain wondered exactly what use the mindless prisoner would be put to. He'd have to ask around and find out. Such knowledge might prove a potent lever to use against Patriccan at some future time.

The ring lowered and darkened in color until only the original yellow disk remained on the floor. Patriccan gestured quickly and the disk, prisoner still encased in the magical barrier, slipped across the floor and out the door like an obedient dog. The mage bowed slightly and took his leave.

"Was it worthwhile, Kiska?"

"It relieved the tensions. I wish you had allowed the torture to continue. This mind burn is too efficient. He babbled all I wanted to know without testing his mettle."

"Testing? Ha. You desired to see only pain. Is your hatred so great that you torture mere soldiers?"

"Yes," she hissed, rocking forward in her chair. "I will do whatever I can to get back at Martak and that filthy creature accompanying him. Anything!"

"Hatred channeled properly is a potent weapon," the man observed. "Can you focus it on . . . other targets?"

An appraising look came into k'Adesina's brown eyes. They softened perceptibly.

"We should study the ways of accomplishing our master's goal."

"Together."

"Definitely. My sleeping quarters are nearby."

"Outside, down the slope and to the left," said Silvain, smiling. This turned into a drama he enjoyed playing to the finish. The woman's energy and hard core of irrational hatred intrigued him. He was driven by personal ambition; what spurred others to equal heights of genius always caught his interest.

To Alberto Silvain's delight, Kiska k'Adesina was able to channel her hatred into other areas. He did not care that there was no love in the coupling. The physical act built, reached a plateau, built more, and then burst in an ecstatic rush that carried them both into still another bout of lovemaking. They finished less than ten minutes before their scheduled midnight meeting with Claybore. Somehow, the nearness of the deadline, the flaunting with the sorcerer's possible wrath, added even more pleasure to the act for both of them.

CHAPTER SIX

"Death awaits all who travel this road," said Jacy Noratumi.

Inyx numbly stared at the area where the overeager soldier had been just seconds before. He had ridden forward, reached that indefinable knife's edge of distortion and . . . vanished.

"What magics can do such a thing?" she muttered. Her mind raced, trying to figure out the spells. On her home world a good clean sword-thrust sufficed. Magic was something left to amuse children; no true warrior used it to kill an adversary—that amounted to cowardice. But since she had walked the Road, the dark-maned woman had seen too many instances like this one.

"Who cares?" Noratumi said bitterly. "I desire nothing more than to enter my fair city once again. A plague on the sorcerer casting this spell! Do you hear, Iron Tongue, a plague on you. May your teeth fall out, may your nose be covered with warts, may your cock turn leprous and send women running from you in horror!"

"Shouting won't get us inside," said Inyx. "And I doubt it's Iron Tongue who is responsible."

"Why do you say that?" he said in a sarcastic tone.

"The grey-clad troops weren't Iron Tongue's. Why do you think this barrier is?"

"Why have both troops *and* magics at work? That is wasteful."

Inyx didn't reply. The people of this world fought different battles than those she was used to. Jacy appeared unconvinced that Claybore would bring forth two types of attack; either that, or his hatred of Iron Tongue was so great that it blinded him to other explanations.

"Who cast it is of little matter," she explained patiently. "Getting past it is more important."

"At last, a logical word from those petallike lips." He lifted himself in his stirrups and bowed, a mixture of sweat and blood dripping from his forehead.

Inyx tried to remember all that Lan had told her of casting spells. He was the expert in this field; she had listened, but had understood only a fraction of what he'd said. It took special talents to be a mage of Lan's caliber, and if the truth be known, the woman was glad she lacked the ability. This war with Claybore changed Lan Martak in ways she liked—and in ways she didn't. He had lost innocence and become more suspicious of all around him.

Confronted with barriers like the one blocking entry into Bron, a touch of paranoia saved lives, however. She had held back long enough to allow the other man to ride ahead to his death, she recalled.

"I cannot remove the barrier or even alter it," she finally said, unwilling to try even the most rudimentary of the spells Lan had taught her. Such an attempt might draw unwanted attention of the sorcerer who had thrown up this magical impediment.

"None of my kingdom dabbles in the black sciences."

"I wish Lan were here."

"Would he fly us up and over this death curtain?"

The bitterness in his voice told more of jealousy than anything else.

"Lan is an accomplished mage. He has stood Claybore's attacks repeatedly."

"Why doesn't he destroy Claybore?"

"Even dismembered as he is, Claybore is a powerful mage. Lan's power grows rapidly, but he can only protect so far. The day comes when he will know enough to launch an attack against Claybore."

"None of this does us any good," complained Noratumi. "Locked out of my own city! This is an outrage!"

The man leaped from his horse and paced back and forth. Inyx watched, but her mind was elsewhere. She knew it wasn't within their power to destroy the deadly curtain veiling them from Bron. Even as she stared at the tiny dust motes leaping about on the road, she saw a firming of the magics. The wavering stopped and was replaced with a vision not unlike peering through fine crystal. The magical barrier was transparent, but Inyx still knew she looked *through* something.

"Damn you, Iron Tongue!" shouted Noratumi. The man picked up a rock and heaved it at the barrier. A tiny puff of smoke came as the rock exploded into a million shards. Another and still another rock followed the first until Noratumi's madness passed. The sallow-faced man panted with the exertion and came back to stand beside Inyx's horse.

His hand rested on her calf. The woman found the gesture strangely disconcerting.

"To have come so far and to be blocked like this. I can't bear it. I cannot!"

"Jacy," she said slowly. "You said there wasn't a mage in your ranks."

"True. We not only scorn them; we fear them for all they've done to our people."

"How do you keep Iron Tongue at bay? Why doesn't

he simply overrun you using a spell and capture the entire of Bron?''

The man turned and sullenly stared at the impenetrable wall of magic. For a moment Inyx worried she hadn't phrased the question properly and had again violated Noratumi's cultural mores. But he was only thinking, not sulking.

''We are fighters. He cannot kill all of us, no matter how good his magic. He knows if he provokes us enough we will launch an attack to the death. Every one of us may die, but so would Wurnna. Not even his golden words can catch us all in one place.''

''So you snipe at one another, Iron Tongue taking a few captives, you killing a few Wurnnans.''

Noratumi shrugged. Inyx knew that such an arrangement benefited only the leaders. It provided a convenient rallying point in case of internal dissension; who dared oppose a leader in the midst of a bitter war? That the war never reached fierce proportions gave even greater strength to Noratumi's position. She guessed Iron Tongue had much the same hold over his people.

''No mages, so we can't break the spell. Using physical means to smash through is not likely. What worries me about even trying is that the effort might attract Claybore's attention,'' Inyx commented.

''This is Iron Tongue's doing,'' insisted Noratumi.

''It is Claybore's,'' countered Inyx. ''His imprint is all over it. No magic, no physical means of ingress possible. Can we fly over it?'' She glanced up in time to see a gerfalcon's wing brush along the surface of the barrier. The bird emitted a shrill shriek of pain, fluttered about, sending down a cascade of feathers, and only managed to swoop away at the last instant before striking the ground.

''Going over does not look promising,'' said Noratumi grimly.

''So we dig.''

"Dig? A tunnel?"

Inyx smiled. It was her turn not to respond. She reined her horse about and headed on a course parallel to the barrier, looking for the proper soil. Digging through rock presented problems she didn't want to face. Loam didn't give a good tunnel. Clay might present the best of all terrains to consider.

"Inyx," came the man's words from behind. She pulled to a halt and waited for him. "Seek not a likely spot."

"Oh?"

Jacy's shoulders slumped and he looked down at the ground, a small boy caught filching candies.

"A way already exists."

"So what are we waiting for? Lead on, Jacy. And do tell me why it is disconcerting to tell me about it." Inyx had visions of deep, dire secrets being revealed. The answer disappointed her.

"I am the leader of all Bron, and first of all time we are miners, workers in stone. This is such an obvious idea it ought to have occurred to me. You are an outsider without . . ." He cut off the sentence abruptly.

"Without what?" she prodded. This was one time she wouldn't let him get away with answering.

"Without proper breeding." He looked up, his amber eyes glowing. "You are the most beautiful woman ever I have seen, but your manners! The way you ask questions shows no sense of decency or rank."

"Ignoring all that, why not just take us to the tunnel so we can get into Bron?"

He heaved a deep sigh, as if saying that this was exactly what he meant about her lack of breeding. Instead, Noratumi motioned for his small group to form up behind Inyx. He vaulted into his saddle and pointed straight ahead. The woman followed the line of his arm and saw only thick undergrowth on a low hill. Jacy trotted past her and let his horse paw at the dirt on the hillside. In a very few minutes the vegetation and a light covering of dirt had been pushed away to reveal a bronze door.

"It leads into the dungeons of Bron. Seldom has it been used. Our founders decided an escape path was required should an attacking army lay siege."

"Now it's providing entrance." Inyx wasn't sure she believed Noratumi's explanation, but it hardly mattered. Several of his men worked to open the massive door. A shaft large enough to ride a horse in gaped open when they had finished.

"Close the door after us," commanded Noratumi.

"What of the concealing vegetation and dirt? Don't you think someone should stay outside to camouflage the entrance?"

Noratumi answered the questions in a roundabout fashion, saying, "The door securely bars from the inside. Since all remaining citizens of Bron are within the protecting walls, there can be no harm in locking it from the inside."

Even as he spoke, an arrow whizzed by to bury its broadhead in a time-dried wooden beam.

"The door! Get it closed!" cried Inyx. She turned in the saddle and stared out the opening. From downhill came a thin line of grey moving out of the forest. Claybore's soldiers had received reinforcements—or not all had been drowned. Where they came from hardly mattered now. That they fired so accurately did. Three of Noratumi's number had fallen under the unexpected onslaught.

The huge bronze door moved with ponderous slowness. Inyx dodged another arrow, jerking away as the fletching grazed her cheek. The door slammed shut with a deafening boom. She heard the echoes travel far down the tunnel.

"I hope this isn't a dead end," she muttered to herself. The warrior woman assured herself the locking assembly on the inside of the door was sufficient to hold back any but the most fervent of attacks, then rode deeper into the hill, following Jacy Noratumi.

The sound of fists pounding impotently against the bronze door trailed her all the way into Bron.

"Now that you have had a chance to relax, would you care for a tour of my lovely Bron?"

Inyx shook her head. They had arrived in the palace dungeons. Getting their mounts up the stone stairs had been a trial, but after that, all had been exactly as Noratumi had promised. Their reception by the remaining citizens within the walls had been little less than tumultuous. Inyx had little taste for such adulation and had pleaded tiredness, and was shown to a sumptuous room in a tower overlooking both the inner city and the valley beyond the walls.

She had taken the opportunity not to sleep but to use an eyepiece obtained for her by the chamberlain to study the movement of the grey-clad troops without. What she had seen didn't please her. More and more gathered around the bronze door in the hillside. Sheer numbers would soon spring open even that sturdy lock. She had no desire to be trapped within the city by the magical barrier and to find Claybore's soldiers boiling up out of the ground like ants.

"You realize that the tunnel will have to be destroyed?" she asked bluntly.

Again came the polite dancing around the issue. Noratumi gazed out the same window she had and said, "When enough of the grey-clads get into the tunnel, it will be flooded."

Inyx nodded, then brushed back a strand of her black hair. That was a wise decision, she knew. Don't just destroy the tunnel. Destroy it in such a way that Claybore had to pay dearly for it.

Not that the mage cared one whit for his men. To

him they were little more than insects doing his bidding. They were expendable in his drive to conquer all the worlds along the Cenotaph Road.

Even as they stood, Inyx felt a rumbling rising up from the very foundations of the city. Noratumi nodded solemnly. The tunnel had been flooded. She closed her eyes and tried not to think of the watery coffin that shaft had become. Somehow, trying not to think of it made it all the more vivid for her. Stone walls. Water rising. Claustrophobia. Horses rearing and throwing riders. Fear. Cries of panic. Water to the waist, the neck, over the head. Bubbles. Lungs exploding. Death.

Cold, lightless, watery death.

"I would see Bron," she said suddenly, wanting to get her mind off the slaughter under the city. "It appears to be a fair city."

"And one to your liking, I should think. Nowhere on this entire world is there a place so hospitable."

As they walked, Inyx came to believe Noratumi's boast. The people greeted not only their leader but her as well. She even thought they would have been cheerful if she hadn't been accompanied by Noratumi.

"How is it," she asked, hoping the question was phrased with proper politeness, "that the leader of Bron leaves his city to go hunting grey-clads in the desert?"

"This empire, this city, is a shadow of its former self," he answered obliquely. "It is because of the spiders in the mountains, the sorcerers in Wurnna, those damnable grey troopers. I rule this empire, and it is my responsibility to defend it."

"You thought you could reach Wurnna with a small, compact guerrilla force, attack from an unexpected direction, and stop Iron Tongue," she said.

"That was the best platoon of fighters I could muster." Noratumi laughed harshly and without humor. "A pitiful handful of fighters. Such has become the glory of Bron. I thought to reach Wurnna and force Iron Tongue into submission. It was a silly gesture. Remaining, keeping my forces to defend Bron from Claybore, that was the proper course. I see it now."

Inyx started to speak, then bit back the words. She hated to tell the embittered man that he was still wrong. It would be impossible to defend Bron much longer. The balance of power between spider, mage, and human had existed for eons on this world. Claybore introduced a new factor, an unsettling one. Simply retreating behind the walls of the city-state meant eventual defeat.

"What is wrong with attempting to parlay? Iron Tongue and the spiders must surely recognize the danger Claybore poses."

"Parlay? With them? Never."

Bullheadedness was nothing new for Inyx. She possessed a fair amount of the trait herself. "Is destruction preferable?" When Noratumi failed to answer, she rephrased the question. "Dying, losing all of Bron forever, cannot be as honorable as negotiating a peace with Iron Tongue to fight a common enemy."

"Allying with Wurnna is no different than petting a scorpion."

"That might be true, but if the scorpion is useful for a short time, use it."

"As it is used, so shall it try to use." The man made a sweeping gesture encompassing all of Bron. "No, this is the way I ought to have done it. Many wiser voices counseled me to fight from a position of strength rather than mounting a weak attack from the desert. They were ever so correct."

"I want to walk around the city—alone, please, Jacy."

He made a vague gesture with his hands, indicating she should do whatever pleased her. Inyx watched as the man walked away, shoulders slumped under the weight of responsibility. He had been different, more vital, alive, when attacking Claybore's troops in Kea

Dell. Now that he faced only defensive battles, Jacy Noratumi's spirit was broken.

Inyx wiped at her nose and turned to hide her emotion. Noratumi could not comprehend the forces arrayed against him by Claybore. She looked over the mighty worked-stone battlements of Bron at the magical sheet barring them from the outside world. That magic provided a better seige than any army with engines of destruction. While the city-state might not be attacked through it, none left Bron.

A week? A month? A year? More? Inyx had no idea how long the citizens might hold out. And it hardly mattered. Claybore had them bottled up and out of the game. One third of the power on this world was immobilized. The spiders—another third—did not matter to the sorcerer. That meant full attention turned against Iron Tongue in Wurnna and the recapture of that precious tongue.

Claybore's full power against a backwater mage already sapped of strength due to decades long warfare with neighbors—the picture turned bleaker by the moment. Inyx realized the only way of escaping a plight identical to that of the others around her was Lan Martak.

"Oh, Lan," she said softly. "I know you cannot hear me, but if you could, know I love you. Once you rescued me from the whiteness between worlds. I need you again to save me from this vile magical imprisonment."

She received no answer, nor had she expected one. Lan and Krek were making their way toward Bron through the mountains. Soon, within days, they would discover the city's predicament and Lan would summon up magics beyond her understanding. Perhaps he might rely on new chants from the master mage's grimoire he carried tucked away in his tunic; or perhaps a simple spell already in his arsenal might suffice.

She hoped he came soon. Already, the walls crushed in on her.

The rest of the day was spent talking with the people of Bron, trying to learn more of their ways, finding that their resolve was strong and that their resources dwindled daily. Simple attrition would bring an end to this once-great city in less than a month.

Inyx walked the battlements looking down into the valley. The river already waned, the industrious creatures building a new dam across the mouth to reform their placid lake. In another week the flow would be properly regulated and all would return to normal. The graves of a hundred or more greys might be exposed to the light of day, but that was small consolation.

Inyx's path led her back to her luxurious quarters in the palace tower. She sat in a chair staring out into space, trying to decide on a course of action and only spinning her mental wheels. She needed divine inspiration.

It did not come.

"Lady, may I bring you some food? It has been hours since you last ate."

Inyx turned dulled eyes toward the servant. The man appeared concerned about her welfare. The least she could do was put his mind at rest.

"I'm not hungry, not now. If anything, the entire city should begin food rationing. With careful doling, we might survive another two months."

"Is it so readily apparent?" the man asked.

Startled, Inyx faced him and said, "I do not pretend to be an expert but I can count both people and supplies in warehouses."

"May I be impertinent, lady?"

She nodded, puzzled at the request.

"Why don't you tell Lord Jacy?"

"He won't listen. He thinks this city impervious to outside forces. In the past, it must have been. But no longer. Claybore is too great a sorcerer; he brings to bear powers learned on a score of other worlds.''

She turned away from the servant and stared at the battlements. Those walls had been constructed four hundred years ago by master stonemasons, one woman had boasted to her. Not once in four entire centuries had they been breached. Inyx started to say something further to the servant, then stopped.

The stone walls surrounding the city began to glow a dull red.

''Look. Tell me what you see. Hurry!''

The servant rushed to her, then shook his head, muttering, ''It can't be. Th-that's not possible!''

The entire wall now glowed red, but one spot near the base turned incandescent. In seconds, molten rock erupted, leaving behind a perfect circular tunnel, through the ten-yard-thick stone wall. Through the tunnel rode grey-clad soldiers, swords swinging and axes humming a death song.

Inyx witnessed the beginning of the end of Bron.

CHAPTER SEVEN

Alberto Silvain stood in the peaceful green valley looking up at Bron. The magnificent pile of stone jutted
against the sky, silently boastful of its strength. Silvain
almost smiled at that ill-conceived vanity. The city
would fall. Soon. He and Kiska k'Adesina had planned
well for the moment.

"Will this be as easy as you claim, Commander?"

Silvain bowed his head and answered his master.

"Bron is a shell. It must be. The land surrounding it
no longer produces foodstuffs to supply it. Water is
plentiful but cannot give full sustenance."

"And," cut in k'Adesina, "their leader's abortive
attack into the desert proves their desperation."

"He fought off Silvain," said Claybore, sarcasm
tingeing his words. Mechanical legs grated slightly as he
twisted about for a better view of the city. Silvain
wondered if the blank eye sockets had to point in the
direction of vision or if Claybore played with his
subordinates, pretending human needs and traits. The
sorcerer's motives were always obscure—and that spurred
Silvain ever onward.

In addition to the power offered him by serving such
a powerful master, Silvain enjoyed trying to decipher

the mage's motives. What good was raw power without continual personal danger to add spice? Silvain lived on a knife's edge with Claybore. One slip and he'd find *his* parts strewn along the Cenotaph Road.

"The company returned to their base after heavy casualties," continued Kiska k'Adesina, unperturbed. In another person, Silvain would have envied her unflappable nature. He had seen strong men quake at the sight of Claybore's fleshless skull and limbless torso. K' Adesina held no fear, because of her obsession with revenge on Lan Martak. That she did not even fear Claybore counted as a mark against her. Silvain believed in intelligent fear and healthy respect.

"You project the conquest of this city to be accomplished in less than a day?"

"Master, given the way into the city, it will be yours within an hour."

"I do not share your optimism, but I do hope you are accurate in your guessing. This city is a thorn in the side, to be removed quickly and as painlessly as possible. Then I may turn my full talents toward Iron Tongue, since he has what I desire most on this worthless world."

"I have studied Wurnna's defenses," said Silvain. "While Kiska turned her strategies against Bron, I formulated an attack plan that even the sorcerers will be unable to turn away."

"Show me." The skull did not look at the map Silvain unrolled. The man put that datum away in his mental file. Claybore's sensory powers bordered on the omniscient. Another thought crossed Silvain's mind. Did the sorcerer know of Silvain's and Kiska's growing physical relationship? Did he approve of it as a way of keeping them both in line? The dangers sharpened Silvain.

"The main defense lies along this canyon. Iron Tongue stands atop a tower and . . . speaks. Armies turn away."

"He uses my tongue."

"Clogging our troops' ears with wax hardly seems adequate since this is a magical and not a physical manifestatiqn. What I propose is as follows." Before Silvain had a chance to continue, a courier came running from the front.

"Speak," commanded the voiceless Claybore.

The youth trembled and nodded, saying, "Master, all is prepared for the final breaching of the wall. Will you give the command?"

"Who casts the actual spell?" asked Claybore.

"Master," said k'Adesina, "Patriccan is ready."

"Then let Patriccan continue."

A motion dismissed the runner, who fled as if the hounds of Hell slavered after him. Silvain and k'Adesina mounted their steeds, readying for battle. The man rested while his mind worked at full speed. This Patriccan and Kiska held a close relationship, that much was obvious. She used him—but what did the mage get in return? There were few enough sorcerers willing to prostitute themselves for Claybore. They tended to be hermits willing to live and work alone in the wilderness for the sake of their black arts. Did Kiska have some hold over Patriccan? A soldier blackmailing a mage? It seemed unlikely. Better to assume Patriccan had his own dark uses for the fragile-seeming Kiska k'Adesina.

And perhaps Silvain might turn that to his own ends.

"I want Lan Martak," the woman said, interrupting his thoughts. The man didn't doubt she would kill anyone between her and the object of her obsession—she might even attack Claybore for the pleasure of slaying Lan Martak.

"My dear, he is yours. The woman, also, if you please. And the spider. I shall keep you from harm while you sate your hunger for revenge."

"It is insatiable. But these deaths will go a long way toward honoring my fallen husband."

They rode to the foot of the hill on which Bron perched. The ancient mage Patriccan held a tiny tube of shiny silver. Seeing the two commanders, he lifted the tube and sighted through it. The entire stone wall began to glow a dim, dark red. Not satisfied, Patriccan reached to the front of the tube and twisted, as if focusing a telescope. The redness remained over the wall, but a single beam of lambent energy lashed forth, striking the wall at its base. Stone bubbled and flowed like stew in a pot. Rock vaporized and the white-hot lance of magic seared through the yards-thick barrier of stone.

Patriccan turned and grandly motioned them toward the city, his job finished.

"Kill them all!" cried Kiska k'Adesina, spurring her mount up the hill. Silvain held back for the briefest of moments, making sure that the protective barrier Claybore had erected to imprison Bron had been removed. The sorcerer was not above sacrificing all his lieutenants for some unguessable end. Sure he did not ride to a magical death at his master's order, Silvain galloped forward until he and Kiska were side by side in the tunnel that had been magically burned through the wall.

Patriccan's cloud had opened the path. The first wave had softened the resolve of those within. Now came the real assault. Silvain and k'Adesina motioned forward a small band of shock cavalry to precede them. Then they prepared to lead the main charge into the city. Their swords tasted the blood. And their combined cries sounded the death knell for Bron.

Inyx peered down from her tower apartment and gasped at the sight. The "feel" of the curtain imprisoning them changed dramatically. Swirling, churning like a tornado, the wall collapsed upon itself—all unseen.

"Chamberlain!" Inyx shrieked, calling for aid, pushing aside the dumbstruck servant. "Alert the city. Get Jacy. They breach the wall."

"Impossible, milady," said the old man. "The wall is a bowshot thick—solid stone. They cannot enter that way."

"Dammit, they're doing it. Oh," she grated, unable to make the man understand. She raced off, sword coming into her hand. By the time she reached the base of the tower and spun out into the courtyard, the spell had hardened into a drill of prodigious power. She saw white-hot gobbets of stone spinning away like some gigantic Catherine Wheel. Inyx threw up an arm to protect her face when the gust of superheated air rushed out from the newly gouged hole through the wall.

From all sides came the pounding of boot soles, men and woman rushing to defend the gaping hole in their defenses. The dark-haired woman hesitated for a moment, studied the scene, then realized that Claybore wouldn't carve such a hole unless the first force through it was truly invincible.

She reached out and grabbed Jacy Noratumi's arm as the sallow-faced man blundered along. He appeared to be in shock. She shook him until his teeth rattled. Only then did the glazed expression begin to fade.

"Inyx," he muttered.

"Don't," she said. "Don't go any further until we see what comes through the hole."

"But we must defend Bron."

"Wait."

Her caution proved their salvation. Those citizens crowding near the still smoking rim of the hole were whisked away like flies on a cow's back when a billowing, churning, all-consuming cloud billowed forth. The magically incited cloud sucked up shrieks of agony and struggling bodies with equal appetite. Only when it emerged fully inside the city walls did the deadly cloud beginning to dissipate. But by then it had done its work.

Inyx hissed, "Listen. Hoofbeats."

"Th-they follow th-that thing." Noratumi's sword quivered as he pointed to the last traces of the deadly cloud. Inyx neither knew nor cared what had spawned the death-dealing vapor. Lan was better able to combat such things. Gripping her sword, she waited for the humans thundering through their tunnel and into the city.

She understood this type of fight. Stance wide, both hands on the hilt of her sword, Inyx readied herself for the first onslaught. The woman glanced to her right and saw that the shock of seeing this city invaded had begun to fade in Noratumi's face. The man finally realized what she had seen from the start; his city was doomed.

"Ha-aieee!" came the war chants of the first rider.

Inyx saw the rider cut through wave after wave of defender, then bear down on her. She waited. Waited. Waited.

Sunlight caught the leading edge of her sword as she swung at precisely the right instant. All the strength locked up in her arms and shoulders went into that cut. Impact jolted her but the meaty feel of sword severing a momentarily exposed wrist was her reward. The rider's gauntlet had slipped and she had taken full advantage of it.

Blood geysering from the stump, the now unseated horseman thrashed about on the ground a few yards distant. Inyx paid him no more attention. He'd bleed to death before he could staunch his wound.

The cavalry surged forward like the ocean's tide. Inyx wiped all thought from her mind and became machinelike, working to swing her sword, parry, duck, retreat, advance. The ebb and flow of the battle lasted forever. She killed attacker after attacker, taking no time to count either victim or time.

Drenched in blood, both from her enemies and from several small but messy cuts, she finally took time to lean forward on her sword, gasping for breath. The riders had pulled back to regroup before making still another frontal assault. Their bravery wasn't in question; Inyx wondered at the fool commanding them. Such wanton squandering of human life was abhorrent to her.

"Inyx," came the distant cry. She turned to find the source and saw that the heat of battle had separated her from Jacy Noratumi. The man stood atop a battlement, crossbow in hand. With methodical skill he aimed, fired, and then handed the crossbow to a squire for recocking while he took another readied weapon.

"Jacy!" she called back, waving. Droplets of blood flew from her sodden sleeve. "Rally your forces. We must escape!"

The man obviously didn't hear. He tossed aside his crossbow and took another, waving to her once more. Vexed, she started to cry out again when some sixth sense warned her of a *presence*.

Inyx turned and looked down the length of the tunnel. A man and woman rode side by side. The woman was unknown to her, but the man she recognized instantly.

"Silvain!"

Inyx rushed forward to gather momentum for her blow. She missed her timing slightly and instantly discarded the idea of going for Silvain's mount. Instead, she turned the line of her attack to the woman at the dark man's side. Inyx swung her sword double-handed and felt the nicked, battle-dulled edge sever a horse's leg. The woman astride the horse never saw the blow. She screamed and went somersaulting through the air.

Silvain reined in, glanced at his fallen companion, and then saluted Inyx before spurring into the main Bron force. He obviously did not care if the fallen woman lived or died. Inyx suspected that to Silvain it was all one and the same.

She'd have to assure herself of a death. The red stripes on the struggling woman's sleeves indicated high rank in Claybore's army. That alone sealed her death warrant.

Inyx lunged, but the woman miraculously turned aside the thrust. It cost Kiska k'Adesina her footing; she went tumbling again, but out of range of Inyx's blade. By the time Inyx had recovered, so had Kiska.

"Now you die, slut," whispered Kiska k'Adesina, advancing with her blade firmly in hand now.

Inyx didn't bother replying. She had already spent her breath on a hard fight. To offer idle taunts would only tire her further. She'd let her sword speak for her. She lunged, in perfect line. The tip of her sword raked along k'Adesina's arm, drawing blood just behind the heavy protective gauntlet.

"Damn you!" cried k'Adesina. "For this you will suffer the same fate as Lan Martak!"

"What?" In spite of herself, Inyx hesitated, surprised at the other's words. "What of Lan Martak?"

"You," said k'Adesina, brown eyes narrowing to slits. "You're his whore. Silvain had shown me a likeness, but the blood hid your identity. Die, bitch, die on Kiska k'Adesina's sword!"

Inyx felt as if she had engaged a tornado in battle. Kiska k'Adesina flew into a murderous rage, her sword coming with unrelenting power. For a time, it proved all Inyx could do to simply stay alive. Tiny cuts became deeper wounds; still she fought a defensive battle. K'Adesina's berserk power carried her onward, no matter what injury Inyx might inflict.

At one point, Inyx managed a deft leg cut, which connected solidly. Kiska k'Adesina appeared not to notice the steady gushing of blood down her leg. Every subsequent step sounded with an almost lewd sucking sound, the foot moving in a blood-filled boot. But it did not stay her rage, her attack, her venomous need to slay Inyx.

Back pressed against the city's wall, Inyx fell into a purely defensive battle. Her earlier fights had tired her too much to deal with such insanity. Her shoulders ached hugely and weakness swept over her in waves as her body demanded tending from all the wounds she had incurred during the past eternity-long minutes of battle.

"Kiska, pull back, let her be," came an all too familiar voice. "Martak isn't within the city walls. We need her alive to find out where he is."

"Kill, kill, kill!" shrieked a wild-eyed k'Adesina. "I will kill that bastard Martak and his animal later. Now I will kill his lover, as he slew mine!"

Everything linked together in Inyx's mind. She knew this woman's identity now; Lan had mentioned the brief encounter with her at the base of Mount Tartanius. Inyx knew she could expect no quarter, now or later. Better to fall in battle with a sword in her hand than to be the subject of intimate tortures by Kiska k'Adesina.

"Kiska, stop, I say. We must find him and the spider."

"Find them yourself. Ever since you failed, you've been trying to curry favor with Claybore. She is mine!"

A whine, a gasp, and Inyx saw her opening. Jacy Noratumi's marksmanship with the crossbow had never been better—or delivered at more precisely the right instant. He had sent a bolt arrowing down into Kiska's sword arm, pinning armored limb to her side. Blood oozed around the quarrel, and not even her rage-insensitivity to pain availed her now. Physically unable to raise her weapon, she had to fall to Inyx's blow.

But before Inyx dealt the killing stroke, she found her blade stopped at the top of its arc by another.

Alberto Silvain bent down from horseback, the tendons in his arm standing in bold relief as he prevented her from killing.

"No, my dear, it is not her destiny to die by your blade." He gritted his teeth and twisted. Inyx's sword spun from her grasp.

"And it's not my destiny to be your prisoner." Inyx dived underneath Silvain's horse, away from his sword. He couldn't swing at her without hitting his own mount. Beneath the man and his mount, Inyx wasted no time. She reached back and grabbed the stallion's huge, dangling member and twisted as hard as she could. The horse let out a cry of pain that sounded almost human. Rearing, bucking, and kicking, the horse tried to rid itself of its assailant.

Inyx continued pressure until she heard Silvain cursing. He'd slipped from his saddle and fallen backwards. Inyx took the opportunity to leap out from her dangerous position, dodging flying hooves as she went. Noratumi's accurate fire with the crossbow from the wall saved her from sure death several times as she ran for the stairs leading up and onto the battlements.

"Hurry," urged Noratumi. "You can make it." She turned blue eyes upward and saw that the man wasn't able to aid her. He had to stay on the walkway and maintain a covering fire if she wanted to reach safety. Gritting her teeth, Inyx fought up one step after another until she lay at Noratumi's feet. The man's fingers bled from continually recocking the bow. Lifting herself on her hands, Inyx saw that Noratumi's squire lay off to one side, his head at an odd angle. A small pool of blood puddled under his fallen body; a few steps further lay one of Claybore's soldiers, a heavy club clutched in his dead hand.

"We must abandon the city," she gasped out. "They have control of Bron now. It's madness to stay and fight them."

"This is my city. I refuse to leave."

"Then' you'll be buried here with every other obstinate fool fighting a lost cause."

"It's not lost," Noratumi muttered, firing the crossbow at another rider below. "It's only a setback."

"Look out there, dammit," raged Inyx, the anger giving her strength. "Half your citizens are already dead. Maybe more. They use sticks and rocks against armored soldiers. And if they happen to prevail, can they withstand another of those magical black clouds? Or even a renewed seige?"

Noratumi said nothing. He stood, fired, cursed, reloaded, and fired again. Inyx surveyed the carnage and wanted to be sick to her stomach. Ankle-deep blood flowed in places throughout the courtyard, eventually finding storm drains to gurgle down. The dead were heaped like refuse. And everywhere the fighting continued, grey-clad against Bron citizen. And everywhere the same distressing story was apparent: Claybore's troops triumphed, slowly, bloodily, but they triumphed.

"I won't be slaughtered, Jacy," she said. "That was Kiska k'Adesina I fought. She wants me with a fervor that goes beyond simple hatred. Her real score to settle is with Lan, but she's not above getting to him through me."

"I stopped her," he said in a tired voice.

"No, you didn't stop her. Slowed her, perhaps, but never stopped. Look. She and Silvain down there are again on the attack. They lost track of me momentarily, but they'll find me again. You can't hold *them* off. Silvain possibly, Kiska k'Adesina never. An hour dead she'll still be fighting."

The words penetrated Noratumi's resolve. "She does not fight rationally. She is . . ."

"Possessed," Inyx finished for him. "If we are to defeat her—and Claybore—we've got to get out of here, regroup, and rethink our attack. Bron is lost, Jacy," she said in a softer voice. "Lost."

He sent a bolt directly for Silvain, but the man's dark eyes spotted the incoming death-messenger, and he batted it aside with a careless swipe of his sword. But the attack had drawn Silvain's unwanted attention. Inyx cringed when he raised his sights to the battlements, smiled, and then called out to Kiska.

"Away, now, Jacy," urged Inyx. "They know where I am."

"This way," said Noratumi, dropping the crossbow and drawing his sword. Inyx followed the best she could, her every muscle aching and her soul weary of the killing. She knocked off one grey-clad soldier and skewered another before joining Noratumi inside a small room hidden inside the thick wall.

"What is this?" she demanded. "I won't be trapped like a sewer rat. Not in here. There's not enough room to even swing a sword."

He said nothing, leaning heavily against a wall. Stone grated against stone and a thick door slowly swung wide. Steps descended into darkness below.

"An escape path," he said. "With luck, others wait for us at the bottom. If not. . . ." His eyes glazed over at the thought of being virtually the sole survivor of Bron.

Inyx didn't need encouragement to start down the stairs. Noratumi closed the door behind, barring it with special wooden wedges. In a larger room below huddled a dozen warriors, caked in blood and scarcely better off than the grey-clads they had killed.

"Where now?"

"That's the difficult part, Inyx," he said, barely looking at the others. "We must make our way outside, across the courtyard, and to the keep."

"No way exists for such an escape," said one of the others. "We're trapped here. Can't get a dozen paces, much less that far."

Inyx peered out a spyhole in the stone wall and saw that

the man spoke the truth. But a plan formed in her mind, one as desperate as it was daring.

"We leave. Now. Follow me."

"Wait, Inyx," cried Noratumi, but the man saw his protest came too late. She had opened the hidden door and exposed them all to danger. Either they followed her or they all died within the walls of Bron. Jacy Noratumi was the last out, and the first to protest Inyx's mad scheme.

"That's death to go in there!"

A quick thrust and Inyx ran through the first soldier she came to. The next guard in the magically bored tunnel was at the other end. Feet padding softly on the stone, she ran hard to reach the other end. The wall seemed to stretch for an eternity, but Inyx found sunlight and blue sky waiting for her at the other end. A quick backhand cut eliminated the guard she found indolently waiting, not expecting any armed retreat back through the tunnel.

"The countryside is ours. Which way, Jacy?"

"Horses. We need horses or they'll ride us down."

Inyx lifted the tip of her sword and pointed toward a crude stall nearby. Silvain and k'Adesina hadn't wanted to enter the city without keeping sufficient horsepower in reserve to carry them to safety if the attack failed.

The small band painfully made its way down the hill to the corral. The more severely wounded were helped by the others. Inyx did a quick count. Only six of the dozen who had joined them would live. The others were doomed, even if the grey-clads didn't overtake them.

"Let's split up," she suggested. "Half go that way and the rest of us down the valley, toward the gap and the crossing canyon."

Noratumi started to protest the folly of dividing their forces, then saw that this was Inyx's way of insuring that the strongest survive by sacrificing the weakest. It tore him apart inside to give the order, but the six worst wounded rode off as decoys while the remaining eight, hardly stronger, rode hell-bent for the dubious safety offered by still another range of mountains.

Even as they rode, the drumming of hooves came from Bron. The pursuit had been joined. The only question was whether or not the other party of wounded gave them enough of a lead to escape.

Inyx doubted it, even as she spurred her horse to more speed.

CHAPTER EIGHT

The mountain arachnids came up the ridge, fanned out in a semicircle and blocking any possible escape. Lan Martak stood with his back against a cliff of cold, cold stone. He looked down into a raging river easily five hundred feet below. It was suicide to jump into that churning, boiling waterway without knowing how deep it was. Even if it were deep enough, the force with which he'd hit the water might be too great. The shock could kill as surely as a knife to the gut.

If he stayed, the spiders got him. Lan made an instant decision, tensed, and took two running steps forward. The third one found only five hundred feet of space beneath him.

He screamed.

He screamed and heard the whispering sounds that were all too familiar to him from long association with Krek. Hardly had the man fallen ten feet when the first of the hunting strands glued itself to his left arm. He turned and jerked, trying to escape it. A second, a third, a tenth all burned against his flesh. He fell another fifteen feet and then snapped to a halt, dangling beneath the spiders.

Helplessly, Lan felt himself being drawn back up.

The thick silvered strands of webstuff were virtually unbreakable. He sawed through one with his dagger, but the others bound him too securely. By the time a second web had parted under his furious assault, the arachnids had him on the ridge once more.

Surrounded by the dozens of spiders towering over him, he simply lay as limp as his shaking body allowed. Amber droplets sluggishly traced their way down the strands and touched his skin. He yelped in pain, then quickly bit back any further sound. The solvent released the hunting strands from his flesh.

Only then did he attempt escape again.

He battered himself against a bristly leg, grabbed hold, and pulled himself to his feet. The spider kicked out, chitonous claw threatening to rip open his guts.

"Sorry, old spider," mumbled Lan as he jerked out his dagger and made a swift cut. He would have hamstrung any mammal. As it was, he only produced a turgid flow from a shallow cut. No damage done, except enraging the spider.

Lan Martak dodged the mandibles clacking shut just inches above his head. Keeping low, he darted in and out between legs until he actually thought he had a chance of winning free.

The hissing as a hunting web wound itself around his legs killed any hope he had.

"No, it won't end this way!" he raged. Lan struggled, then calmed. He hated the idea of using magic against these creatures who were so much like his friend, but survival depended on it. His personal life meant nothing in the worlds-spanning struggle against Claybore; but if he died, all hope of defeating the dismembered sorcerer died with him. The fate of worlds depended on him, yet he couldn't bring himself to employ a fire spell against his captors. Wanton slaughter like that might please Claybore; Lan was better than the sorcerer he fought

across the universe. If he didn't live up to his own
ideals, why fight at all?

A small spell, the fire conjuration took hardly any
concentration. But Lan put everything he had into it.
He felt the sparks dancing along his fingertips.

"He burns!" cried one of the spiders separated from
the scene. "Stop him or he will set us all aflame!"

The spiders' fear of fire matched Krek's. Angry hissing sounded and Lan felt hundreds of tendrils strike his
body, spin him around, encapsulate him. The fire burned
sluggishly at his fingers and he found himself unable to
bring it into full-raging heat as long as his arms were
pinned. Claws turned him about, stood him upright,
and then came the real cocooning. Hissing, whispering
softly, the webs fell about his body, layer upon layer
until only his face remained free.

"Don't cover my nose and mouth," he begged.
"You'll suffocate me."

The arachnids argued among themselves about how
far to go in the cocooning process. At last they decided
Lan presented no further danger to them, either magically or physically. They allowed him to keep his face
free.

"Watch it!" he cried, as he felt his feet yanked out
from under him. He landed heavily, bruising his shoulder even through the cushioning cocoon.

A web lashed to his feet dragged him down the side
of the mountain. By the time they reached the valley,
Lan regretted that the spiders hadn't simply killed him.
Every joint and muscle in his body had been bruised
and strained. Uttering small numbing spells helped him
for a while, but the use of the magic grew too tiring; he
fought against the red tide of pain washing against his
consciousness and threatening to drown him.

He rolled over in the dust of the valley floor and got
a fair look around him. Dozens of spiders remained on
patrol not twenty yards distant. Even if he could use his

fire spell without seriously burning himself before the
cocoon strands parted, the spiders would be on him in
an instant, added webs weighing him down until no
hope remained.

"There has to be some other way. But what? What?"

The man's mind raced. The fire spell kept returning
to be the one most potent against the spiders, but its use
was limited by his desire for self-survival. And Lan
Martak hated to use the spell if it appeared he was
going to die; such retribution accomplished nothing in
the present circumstances. It certainly would do little to
fight Claybore.

"A spell," he said to himself. "Cold? No good.
None of the others is easily done, either." He wished
he could reach the grimoire carefully tucked away
under his tunic. The spells therein might hold the key to
his escape. But with arms pinned and the grimoire
securely bandaged inside the cocoon he might as well
have wished for total release.

Two of the spiders trotted over. One of them spoke.

"You have been chosen for an honor totally unwor-
thy of you, human."

"What's that?"

"Food for the Webmaster's hatchlings. Hoist him
aloft."

Lan Martak screamed as the strand around his feet
tightened. He felt himself rushing upward into the sky,
feet first. His forehead brushed the ground for the
briefest of instants and then he dangled head down fifty
feet in the air. Lan controlled his triphammering heart
and tried to relax. It wasn't easy suspended so far above
the valley floor.

Lan Martak felt the sticky strands around his ankles
quiver and shake as if some huge being nibbled at his
flesh. The involuntary movement on his part caused a
slight swing. He got an unwanted view of the valley,

the web from which he dangled, and the sides of the canyon. And on one slow circuit he saw a spider slowly making its way toward him along the aerial pathway.

He swallowed hard, trying not to panic. His magic had availed him little. Without the use of his hands he couldn't properly conjure. At one point he had even decided it was better to die in flames than to hang here awaiting dozens of hungry spiderlets—but he hadn't been able to conjure up the fire spell at all.

Now they came for him. To eat him. Pieces slashed off and fed to newborns.

He might live for days before finally perishing.

The spider came closer and closer, Lan only getting brief glimpses as he swung to and fro faster and faster, due to the added weight on the web holding him.

"You appear distraught, friend Lan Martak. There is no need," came the familiar voice. "I am not the one who will eat you."

"That doesn't make me feel any better, Krek."

"It ought to. Not every human is destined to be dinner for future Webmasters." Krek looped strands of his own sticky web material about the existing web and dropped so that he stared Lan in the eye. The human felt a surge of vertigo. For the spider, this was a perfectly natural way of conversing. What did it matter if one or both of the parties was upside down?

"I don't want to be dinner for anyone, much less a hatchling of some damned Webmaster."

"I am a Webmaster," Krek pointed out gently. "But far removed from my domain." Lan thought the spider was going to cry as he launched off on still another bout of nostalgic yearnings. "It seems that Murrk has hit upon what is the ideal situation. You see, his mate desired to devour him, as was her right and duty, but he convinced her that better nutrition lay in cocooned humans. An elegant solution to a problem, one that never occurred to me. After all, humans do taste funny. 'Tis a true pity I am not back in my Egrii Mountains with such a notion. Klawn and I can be reconciled. Ah, my lovely, petite Klawn.''

"You'll never see that domain again if you let them eat me.''

"Why not? I walked the Road long before meeting you. While my plight was different then, it is no less perilous now. Imagine, a Webmaster of the Egrii Mountains, lost amid worlds, spurned by his own mate, combating evil. 'Tis the stuff of legends, but living it is less than happy for me. With Webmaster Murrk's solution, my dilemma might be soluble after all.''

Lan said nothing, composing his thoughts to argue with the alien brain. Krek was his friend, but the spider did not think like a human. To him being eaten was a fact of life, even if it was a fact he so cravenly ran from.

"What of this place?'' asked Lan, changing his tactics. Any information gleaned about his arachnid captors might suggest ways of freeing himself from this heels-over-head predicament. "Have you spoken with the spiders about Claybore?''

"They know of him and the grey-clad soldiers he brings, but they count them as of little importance.''

"What? But they can't. Claybore's dangerous!''

"To these fine spiders, he is only another human. I can appreciate their problem in discerning the difference between a skull and torso riding a mechanical contrivance and an ordinary human. The similarities are ever so obvious. One head, an insufficient number of appendages, no mandibles or sleek, furry legs.''

"Can you rally them against Claybore?''

"I do not believe that is possible. Not in the sense you mean. To fight against Claybore and his troops if they enter this valley, yes. They will do that. To sally forth and do battle elsewhere, never. Or at least not unless the situation changes dramatically. It is difficult enough protecting this valley from the sorcerers in Wurnna.''

''Wurnna?''

''Where this Iron Tongue rules. He makes life most deplorable in this valley, what with his raids and ugly spells. The locals do not like him one bit.''

''Why does Iron Tongue even enter this valley? What's here that draws him so?'' Lan felt lightheaded from so much talking. Dangling upside down did nothing to improve his circulation or disposition.

''Here, nothing. But on the far end of this mountain range, in spots reached only by traveling this valley, seem to be mines of some sort. Murrk knows that the humans imprison their own kind and ofttimes even kill them in pursuit of whatever is locked within the ground.''

Lan frowned. Was gold or silver so important that the wrath of the spiders was dared?

''Murrk is the Webmaster?'' he asked.

''Oh, yes, a fine specimen. So regal, even royal in appearance, as befits a Webmaster.'' Krek vented a gusty sigh that caused the entire web to bounce from side to side. The effect on Lan was even more pronounced. The man closed his eyes and imagined he was aboard a wind-powered sailing ship pitched on twenty foot waves. It didn't help his churning stomach settle down.

Lan gasped out, ''Stop moving. I . . . I'm getting sick.''

''Well, mage, heal thyself,'' the spider said primly. ''I rather enjoy the sensation of being once more in a decent-sized web, a hundred feet above the ground, feeling the gentle zephyrs wafting through the fur on my legs, tingling and ever so lightly teasing. *That* is a sensation second to none.''

''I'm going to be sick.''

''Do not despoil the landscape, friend Lan Martak. Murrk would not approve. He is most jealous of preserving this terrain for posterity.''

Lan had to fight down the rising wave of nausea and almost gagged. But life or death hung in the balance. That thought entered his head and he started to laugh at the unintentional pun. Hung in the balance. Harder and harder he laughed, until hysteria seized control.

It was a more difficult battle fighting down this fear-fed laughter than it had been the physical upset.

"You take this setback hard, friend Lan Martak."

"Krek, can you get me down from here? We've got to escape this valley. If . . . if you like, you can return, but I must get away and find Inyx and the others. Fighting Claybore is all I want to do. It's what I *must* do."

"Come back? Why would I do a silly thing like that?"

"But I thought you liked it here. The way you've been talking, I thought you . . ."

"Murrk is Webmaster. I cannot remain in the company of spiders at less than my former rank. It is too demeaning. As long as he rules this valley, I am merely a traveling dignitary. For me to stay is out of the question. Lan Martak, you say the most peculiar things."

"Then *get me down*!" Lan's temper flared. His outburst caused the bobbing motion again. For once he silently thanked Murrk for hanging him so far above the ground. Up here there was no chance of banging his head on the ground.

"It is not that simple. I thought I had adequately explained it to you."

"Explained what? Get me down!"

"You are only a small victim in the war between spiders and humans on this world. Whatever is mined from the ground is very important to Iron Tongue and the others of Wurnna. They desecrate the valley, threaten spiderlings, even use fire to drive warriors away. Such high-handedness is not to be tolerated."

"What could they be mining?" mused Lan. This

entire world remained at war, no matter if Claybore were added into the equation or not. Spider fought human, whether from Bron or Wurnna it made no difference. Jacy Noratumi fought Iron Tongue for imprisoning his subjects. And now Lan knew that Iron Tongue used those slaves from Bron in mines.

"Murrk says the stone glows in the dark. Is that of any real importance?"

"I have never heard of a rock doing that, at least not without either phosphorescent moss or slime on it. Or an ensorceled rock."

"Why would anyone place a spell on all the rock coming from a single location? If Iron Tongue desired that, why choose stone from a region guarded by my fellow arachnids?"

"Those aren't questions I can answer dangling like this, Krek. Free me. Let's run for the end of the valley."

"We would be stopped within yards. Murrk is doubling the number of his patrols. Claybore and the grey-clads march constantly in the direction of Bron, and the Webmaster does not like such intrusions."

"Bron will fall soon. Inyx is in danger."

"I fear you are correct, friend Lan Martak. Friend Inyx has chosen a dangerous path, unlike ourselves."

"There's no danger to you, dammit!" snapped Lan. Regreting his outburst, he soothed the spider by saying, "We must aid Inyx. Only we can do it. You with your strength and me with my magics."

"My intelligence is important, also."

"Yes, that," Lan said patiently.

"And my devastating grasp of tactics."

"And your fighting prowess. Yes, all of those. Now how do you propose to get me down from here?"

"Eh? Oh, I suppose it behooves me to go speak with Murrk about this. His hatchlings won't be hungry enough for a complete human for several days."

"How comforting."

"I thought it would ease your mind." Krek walked up his web and gained the main strands, striding off in a gait that was the epitome of grace. On the ground his eight-legged, rolling motion appeared awkward. In this aerial world of webs, he was perfectly suited for smooth, swift movement.

Lan Martak hoped Krek did not forget his stated purpose of freeing him. The thought of hungry spiderlings caused cold sweat to bead on his forehead. And worst of all, he couldn't even wipe it off.

Krek approached the Webmaster and hung in the web at a respectful distance. By human conventions, they remained motionless for an impolite time; by arachnid standards, Krek hurried the conversation almost to the point of rudeness.

"Webmaster Murrk," he began. The other spider twitched slightly, indicating his distaste for such precipitous behavior, but Krek wasn't to be swayed. Something of his human friend's desperation had taken seed within him. To leave this pleasant valley bordered on the absurd, since he had searched world after world along the Road for such a wonderful place filled with his own kind, but other important duties had overtaken him in those wanderings.

Inyx. The spider thought carefully about the dark-haired woman whose manner differed so from other humans. She was almost bearable at times and the thread of bloodthirstiness in her pleased the spider. He understood her more than he understood the others, especially Lan Martak.

Lan. His powers grew at a pace none comprehended, much less the man himself. Krek's unspiderly abruptness with Murrk was fueled by those powers. Claybore presented a clear and present danger, but Lan's own untried, untrained powers seemed as much a hazard.

Allowing his friend to remain cocooned and dangling only added to the magical problems. By accident Lan Martak might hit upon a spell to free himself. The consequences of destroying this valley and all the gallant, noble beings within it made Krek shiver with horror. Rescuing Lan and rejoining Inyx outweighed any consideration of further enjoyment of this fine, restful resort area.

"Webmaster Murrk," he said again, "there are problems in the web."

This formal declaration brought the other mountain spider about to peer eye to eye with Krek.

"The web is my only concern," he responded ritualistically.

"The being you hold for your hatchlings is not as he seems."

"It seems fit fodder. It will not poison my hatchlings?"

"Doubtful," Krek said honestly. "There are other possibilities, however, all of which must be examined. He summons powers he can barely control. If he does so, consciously or unconsciously, all within the web are doomed."

"He is one of those living there?" Murrk twitched his second right leg in the direction of Wurnna. "They prey on us. We eat them when they become careless. But never have they displayed the kind of power you prattle on about."

"Their powers are different. Lan Martak travels the Road and accumulates odd bits and pieces of lore in a distressingly helter-skelter fashion." Krek saw this did not impress the Webmaster. He changed his tack. "Those of Wurnna do not command as great a power."

"They do not dangle wrapped in my cocoon, either. Some power. Get on with this." The terseness told Krek his welcome had been overstayed.

"My feeling is that this human is best released. I will guarantee he will never again return to this valley."

"After my hatchlings dine, I will make the same guarantee."

Krek bobbed his head and swung back into the web, tracing through the traverse lines that were not coated with web-glue for trapping prey. He climbed toward the sun, feeling its warmth soaking into his body, giving strength, firming his resolve. Life had become confusing with Lan Martak. Values held for a lifetime sloughed away like a snake's used skin. To question another Webmaster's decision was unthinkable—yet Krek thought it.

Murrk did not have the full facts. He ignored Claybore's obvious menace. Krek realized with a sudden flash of insight how insular most spider colonies were. Their world consisted of the web and the terrain around it. And as long as the arachnids remained on high, this was enough.

It was he who had changed, not the others of his kind.

"Oh, friend Lan Martak, what have you done to me? I question now when before I acted according to instinct." The spider heaved a sigh that sent vibrations throughout the web. Others glanced up and saw him, then went about their own business. Krek bemoaned the insanity that had seized him. The insatiable urge to see new worlds. The shirking of his duty at mating time. The desire to aid the humans in their fight against Claybore and his grey-clad legions. All insanity. And now, all his.

Krek spun about and, head-first, plunged toward the earth. At the last possible instant, he slowed his progress with a few well-chosen gobbets of webstuff. When his talons touched dirt, he felt no shock of the fall at all. He looked neither left nor right. He had decided on the proper course of action.

Above dangled Lan Martak.

"Krek, are they going to release me?" came the plaintive question.

"Webmaster Murrk is intent upon feeding you to his hatchlings. He avoids his husbandly duties in this fashion, an interesting concept: Provide enough for the hatchlings and perhaps full conjugal responsibility can be deferred."

"I don't care if his mate eats him or not!" bellowed Lan. "I don't want to be served up as dinner to a wiggling horde of spiders!"

"Do calm yourself, friend Lan Martak. In the course of my conversation with Murrk, he mentioned that Wurnna is a short distance away." Krek lifted a leg indicating the appropriate direction. "Once freed, you can find safety in that city. Those living in this valley are not aggressively inclined towards any but stragglers from Wurnna, Bron and the occasional grey soldier."

"Once I'm free?" asked Lan. "But you said Murrk wasn't—"

"Please," said Krek, beginning the climb up a canyon wall. "This is difficult for me. I feel as if I betray all my own kind, but it seems necessary, given the problems you have brought down upon your own head." Drops of amber appeared on Krek's mandibles. The solvent touched strands of Lan's web. The helpless man shrieked as he plunged headfirst for the hard ground.

Krek neatly snared him with a hunting web inches before he smashed to his death.

"Now for the difficult part. Each spider produces a formula of his own for cocooning. Only familial lines are entitled to know the precise composition of the silk. This prevents the less scrupulous of those in our web from filching food stored away. However, I believe finesse is not required."

Lan shuddered at the nearness of Krek's mandibles as they slashed and hacked at the tough cocoon. It took almost ten minutes for the last imprisoning strand to be stripped away. Standing shakily, Lan grasped one of Krek's firmer front legs.

"Thanks, old spider. Lead the way out of here. We can be in Wurnna by nightfall if we hurry—and if Murrk was right about the distance."

"He was right. He is, after all is said and done, a Webmaster. We Webmasters do not make elementary errors like that. However, since this escape is against his wishes, I feel it best for you to press on without me. I shall remain behind to placate Murrk."

"But Krek, he'll kill you!"

"Why?"

"But you helped me escape. He has to know."

"I didn't eat you for myself. That is a potent argument I shall use to sway him into a truce. If it is impossible to form an alliance, then nonintervention is the next best course of action."

"Krek, you'll be killed if you stay behind."

"If you do not begin your own escape immediately, you will once again be cocooned for a spiderling's late supper. I shall forge the link with Murrk, then join you in Wurnna. As you know, I can traverse the distance much more quickly than you." Krek's expression didn't change, but the tone came out as a sneer. "After all, I have an adequate number of legs to carry me."

"Don't be long," said Lan. He squeezed down on Krek's leg one last time and began down the path as fast as he could. Krek watched until his friend had vanished from sight, then turned and bounded into the web to once more seek an audience with Webmaster Murrk.

Krek wondered if Murrk would eat him or not. If the situation were reversed, Krek knew what he'd do.

CHAPTER NINE

Exhausted, feet bleeding and hands ripped from the sharp rocks he'd been forced to climb to escape the floor of the valley, Lan Martak almost collapsed when he saw the small hunting party ahead on the narrow trail. He sank to the earth and slumped so that his back was braced on a flat slab of dark red granite, then waited. Sucking in painful chestfuls of air, he scented the pungent mountain juniper and other smells less identifiable. After all, this wasn't the world of his birth; he moved too quickly between worlds now to fully appreciate the diversity and similarity. Living off the land had been difficult, and if he hadn't found a large dam holding back the main waters of the river running through the valley of spiders, he would have had almost no food. But watercress failed as important sustenance in his belly and there had been nothing else he didn't judge as poisonous.

Tightening his hands into fists, he pushed himself upright and listened for the telltale scrapings of feet against rocks. He knew the humans in the hunting party couldn't miss him; he prayed that they would ask questions first before killing.

They circled him, bows carried with arrows nocked and ready to fly into his body.

"I mean you no harm," Lan said. He blinked in surprise when it occurred to him that his voice came out croaking and weak, barely audible. The flight from the valley of spiders had taken more out of him than he'd thought. "Iron Tongue," he said through cracked lips. "I want to see Iron Tongue."

The men exchanged glances and shook their heads, saying nothing. Lan closed his eyes and leaned back, the cold rock sucking away his body heat. He reached within and found the proper places to touch with his magics. As he had done in the past, he summoned forth extra strength. The penalty later would be greater due to his weakened condition now, but Lan knew he had no choice. If he did not convince these hunters to aid him, he was dead anyway.

"Stop!" came a command from out of his range of vision. Lan painfully twisted about and stared upward. A woman, dark, loose hair blowing in the wind whipping along the ridge, stood with arms crossed. She wore a hide shirt decorated with feathers and streamers of orange and yellow silk. Tiny bits of silver caught and reflected the waning sun and made Lan squint slightly.

The archers relaxed, but they kept their arrows only an instant away from deadly flight into his aching body.

"He uses magic," the woman said. "Does any here recognize him?"

"None, Rugga," answered the man off to one side. "He is not of Wurnna."

"I walk the Road," Lan said. His voice strengthened as he forced the power from within to flow smoothly. He struggled to his feet, but he had to keep one hand against the granite facing. The strength he now "borrowed" magically would soon flee. "I escaped the valley of the spiders. I seek Iron Tongue."

"So you said," the woman above called. "Why do you want him?"

Lan swallowed bile rising from inside and controlled his own lightheadedness. He had the sinking sensation that he had been found by a group at odds with the ruler of Wurnna.

He had no choice. He had to pursue this line or soon he'd be unable to follow any.

"We have a common enemy. Claybore and his grey-clad legions."

"And not also the spiders?"

"I have no quarrel with them, though they did try to eat me."

The woman laughed. It wasn't a pleasant sound.

"They eat many of our rank. It seems that Iron Tongue refuses to let me eradicate them once and for all. They serve some purpose which he refuses to reveal to a mere sorcerer, such as myself."

"He uses them as an excuse to enslave other humans," muttered one of the hunting party.

"Silence, fool." Rugga came more fully into view for Lan, then simply stepped out into thin air. Instinct forced his leaden arms aloft to catch her, but it wasn't necessary. The woman floated downward as if following a drifting feather. And as light as that feather, she touched rock only a pace from Lan Martak.

"You have endured much," she said, cool, gray eyes working over his body. "Once you were quite handsome. But now." She shrugged.

"I have been through much."

"Cocooned, from the look of your clothing." Slender fingers reached out and tugged at bits of the web still clinging to his garments. Those fingers lingered for a moment before leaving. Where Rugga had touched him the flesh warmed and came alive.

"You are a mage," he said.

"There are few enough of us left, no thanks to Iron

Tongue and his ambitions. We do what we must to survive.''

''If it weren't for Rugga, we'd be . . .'' began one of the hunters. A cold gaze from the woman froze the words in his throat. He averted his eyes and shuffled back a few paces.

''My hunters abuse their privilege of speech away from Wurnna.''

Lan took in all he saw and heard and came to unsatisfying conclusions about these people. These were not free men; while not slaves, they were under close supervision with independent thought and action discouraged strongly. Rugga, while not supporting Iron Tongue, did little to change the man's rules. Iron Tongue ruled Wurnna. Rugga obeyed, reluctantly.

''I don't wish to seem abrupt, but I'm not feeling well,'' he said, a veil of black slipping down over his eyes. Lan fought but his knees buckled. A strong arm supported him—Rugga's.

''Help him, fools. We return to the city immediately.''

''But we haven't finished the hunt. Iron Tongue won't approve. The siege. We need the food!''

''Silence!''

Even half-unconscious, Lan felt ripples of power blasting forth in that word. Rugga used magic to control her minions. He slumped all the way into oblivion, his head resting against the woman's breast.

Lan Martak came to, instantly alert. The aches and pains in his body were history. He had never felt more alive in his life. He sat bolt upright and peered about him. Rugga sat tailor-fashion a few feet away, working on a succulently roasted leg of some game fowl. Of the other hunters, he saw nothing.

''They scout ahead. Claybore has Wurnna under seige,'' she explained, then she returned to eating. But the gray eyes never left Lan. He felt as if she stripped the flesh from his bones and examined the skeleton in minute detail.

"How long has it been? Since you found me?"

"A day. Perhaps a day and a half." She smirked at his expression. "My magics are as powerful as yours. I had never seen the strength-giving spells used in quite the way you tried. The application had a curious combination of adroitness and inefficiency. I improved on it."

"How?" Lan expressed real curiosity. This was the first chance he'd had to question a practicing mage. The others he'd met had either been hostile, like Claybore, or obsessed with their own particular projects. "My grasp of such things is limited."

"You're self-taught?" This obviously startled Rugga. She covered it by saying, "In a manner of speaking, all sorcerers are self-taught. The spell works like this."

She began a low, haunting chant, weaving the elements of Lan's strength spell with other, different spells. The man followed the lines of magic, tracing them, letting them insinuate themselves into his brain until he understood.

"Very nice," he complimented. The smile he got in return told him that Rugga thought he meant something other than the effectiveness of the spell. Looking at her with refreshed vision, Lan decided his words covered all aspects. Rugga's feather- and silk-decorated shirt hung open at the front, the laces loosened to allow him to see the warm white breasts pressing forward. As she casually tossed away the remains of her dinner, he caught flashes of pink cresting the peaks.

The woman was fully aware of him and his appraisal. She lounged back, supporting herself on one elbow, long, slender legs thrust out. A deep green fabric clung to her thighs and calves with static intensity. Ankle-high boots of soft brown leather form-fitted her feet, giving her the ability to walk quietly and surefootedly on the rocky trails. About her slender waist hung a simple pouch fastened with a thong of leather wrapped around a large bone button.

"The others have gone ahead," she repeated. "We are quite alone."

Lan felt subtle tugs of magic. Her allure was undeniable, but Rugga enhanced it with a spell. With a single wave of his hand he brushed away the imprisoning magics.

"Not that way," he said, holding down his anger. "None uses magic to sway me."

Her thin eyebrows arched. "You are the first to ever notice my spell. I am growing clumsy in my old age." Her eyes hardened, then she added, "Or I have never before met a mage of your prowess. You are wrapped in contradiction, my friend."

"Wurnna. I must go to Wurnna and meet Iron Tongue."

"He is so important? When we can . . . dally here?"

This time the only attraction Lan felt was purely physical. Rugga used no spell on him.

"A few hours seems less important to me than it once did," he said. She rose like a hunting panther and slipped down beside him. Her arms crushed him even as her lips worked feverishly against his. Lan felt a spell being cast, but this one he did not fight. It enhanced his physical prowess, made every nuance of their touch more vital, more exciting. He even learned the spell and returned it to Rugga, to the woman's obvious delight.

It was almost sunset before they started on the trail for Wurnna.

"I feel it," Lan Martak said softly. "The very air quivers with magic."

"So it has been since Claybore found this planet. Iron Tongue refuses to do more than counter the spells, but he holds the grey-clad soldiers at bay."

"How does he do that?"

Rugga stared at the man in disbelief.

"He is Iron Tongue. When he speaks, all others obey." A sly smile crept over her thin, lightly rouged lips. "But you will learn more about this soon. Now be quiet. We approach the fringes of Claybore's troop encampment."

They walked in silence for ten minutes, signs of soldiers all around. Rugga held up a finger to caution Lan to even greater care, but he did not need the warning. He saw the camp stretching around the bend in the rocky canyon. Fully a thousand soldiers plugged the escape from Wurnna.

Rugga walked onward confidently, not even glancing toward the soldiers marching their posts. Lan felt the hairs on the back of his neck rise. Whatever spell Rugga cast caused the sentries to turn and glance in the opposite direction whenever the pair passed nearby. Rounding the canyon elbow, Lan caught sight of Wurnna in the distance. The entire city glowed a dull blue.

"Yes," said Rugga in hushed tones. "Claybore's magic. The soldiers remain hidden but the magic is impervious to Iron Tongue's persuasiveness. However, Claybore's mages cannot get close enough to apply the spells fully."

"A standoff?"

"One that Iron Tongue permits to exist."

"Why? Why doesn't he do something? Why send out hunting parties for food, when they could act as guerrilla bands? Why . . ."

"Iron Tongue's motives are his own. He turns this siege into a reason for his continued power. If anything, his authority has grown since Claybore's coming."

"They work together?"

A harsh, curt laugh was his answer. Lan Martak considered the woman's words. He knew nothing of Wurnna and Iron Tongue, but he did know something of human nature. Iron Tongue had built himself into supreme authority through the use of the tongue and now maintained his position because of the dangers posed by Claybore's army. No one lightly relinquished such power; as long as the threat persisted, Iron Tongue's position was secure. It was a dangerous balancing act, magic against magic, lives hanging in the balance, but one probably worth it when considered from the ruler's standpoint.

"The challenge," Rugga said. Lan felt intense heat beneath his feet. Rugga's hands moved swiftly and she muttered the counterspell. The rocks cooled suddenly and she motioned him toward a solid stone wall. "Our entrance."

Lan hesitated, then *felt* the stone changing. Once it had been solid. Now it turned into mist. He walked forward *through* the stone. Even as he passed, the wall stiffened into impervious rock once again.

"An effective spell, but one which must drive your architects to desperation."

"True, they don't get to use their decorative skills on the external walls, but they are given free rein inside Wurnna. Witness!"

Lan stopped and drank in the beauty of this sequestered city. Towers of feathery grace soared upward, impossibly fragile. Crystals of phosphorescent green and red and orange embedded in the streets glowed with enough intensity to permit travel at night. Everywhere he looked he saw delicate beauty.

"The architects outdo themselves," he admitted. But Lan also noted the populace. Amidst such splendor none smiled. No one joked along the gorgeous thoroughfares. Children shuffled along, heads down, as if being punished for some crime. Adults moved with suspicious glances at all around.

"The people do not appreciate all Iron Tongue has done for them," Rugga said, her words tinged with sarcasm.

"Is he so powerful?"

"Come. I shall take you to him and allow you to see for yourself." Rugga smiled, as if at some small joke she did not choose to share. "You will understand. Oh, yes, dear Lan, you will soon understand."

They walked swiftly, Lan setting the pace. He felt the chill of fear knifing through the people. The beauty became that of a tomb imprisoning spirit and the obvious wealth, a thing to be despised.

"Here. Iron Tongue." Rugga pointed at a simple building a hundred paces distant. "I must leave you now. He will see you."

"You're not coming with me?" Lan felt a sudden surge of irrational panic.

"He doesn't desire my presence now any more than he has in the past. I go to my quarters. After he finishes with you, come by. Anyone can direct you." The long, slender fingers brushed his cheek. Again he felt the heat of her light touch. A smile curled her lips, but it wasn't a pleasant one. Rugga silently turned and strode off, head high, shoulders back, feathers and bangles whipped backward by the force of her departure. Lan had the feeling she had just left him with his executioner.

Magic permeated the atmosphere, just as fog dampens the skin and sometimes condenses to run in tiny rivulets. Lan Martak walked slowly toward the simple arched doorway; as he walked, the pressure of varying spells worked against him. He cast some aside. Others he recognized and neutralized. He had a native ability to sense magic, but only recently had found power to cast his own spells.

He entered the building and found cool darkness. Light vanished totally in front of him and only a dim outline of the archway was cast. He closed his eyes and trusted other senses. Tiny rustlings of silk and silver came from his left. He moved in that direction. Tiny hints of perfume dilated his nostrils, even as someone coughed genteelly. Lan imagined the cough captured by a lacy handkerchief.

"Iron Tongue?" he asked, stopping when he felt a *presence* nearby. "I come to enlist your aid against Claybore."

"Lan Martak," came the deeply resonant voice. "I am happy to see you. You bring joy to this house. My city welcomes you as a potent enemy of my enemy."

Lan opened his eyes. Lights had blossomed and shone down on the man seated upon an ornately carved wooden throne. Tucked into one of the man's sleeves was a handkerchief identical to the one Lan had imagined—or had it been more than imagination in this magic-infested place?

"I fight Claybore across many worlds."

"And with great success," Iron Tongue broke in. Lan felt prickles of magic tugging at the fringes of his mind, elusive and distant, but potent nevertheless. "I choose to sit and allow him to batter himself against Wurnna's defenses. He cannot enter. The mages of Wurnna are allied against him."

The words carried no real meaning. The undercurrents soothed Lan, fed his ego, made him believe only Iron Tongue could aid him in his battle with Claybore. The man moved closer and watched as Iron Tongue stiffened defensively. Lips parted slightly allowed a ray of light to shine against a dark round tongue in his mouth.

Iron. And magically endowed.

Lan began weaving counterspells both against what he felt and what he suspected. Iron Tongue talked more earnestly; pressures mounted. The battle of wizards turned out to be at an almost subconscious level, but all too real for Lan.

One misstep and he fell under this man's verbal domination.

"Rugga says you escaped from the valley of spiders. A feat of courage second to none in the annals of Wurnna." Again meaningless words but carrying a shock-charge of magic intended to reduce Lan's will and subjugate him.

"What is it you mine in their valley?" Lan asked. His question carried an attack of his own, weaving in and out of Iron Tongue's own offensive thrusts.

"The power stone, of course. We use it to give life to Wurnna. The streets glow from it. The towers soar because of it. The very defenses that hold Claybore at bay depend on it."

Lan began hardening his own attack. He delighted in the play of magics and the feeling that he held his own with such a potent mage. It was this confidence that emboldened him to risk more daring spells, ones he had only considered and never given life to.

"The power stone is mined by slaves captured from Bron," Iron Tongue went on. Sweat beaded his forehead now. "Workers, rather. *Willing* workers."

"Slaves," said Lan.

"Slaves." The word came from between clenched lips. "I require the threat of the spiders to justify the slaves." Iron Tongue stiffened visibly and sweat poured down his face. Lan's spell tightened like a noose about him.

"You can sue both Bron and the spiders for peace. Forge an alliance against a common enemy."

"NO!" roared Iron Tongue. The blast issuing from his mouth staggered Lan. Madness and magic mixed with rationality. For the briefest of instants, he lessened his spells. This was all Iron Tongue required to recover his composure. "You will make a worthy ally," the ruler said, with some sincerity this time. Lan felt nothing of the verbal pressures that had accompanied the other statements.

"We are not enemies. I do not approve of your policies, but we are not foes. We both fight Claybore."

"Rugga has gotten to you, I see," said Iron Tongue, sighing. "She is most persuasive, in her own fashion."

"There is nothing in—" Lan began. He cut the sentence off in the middle. The word-fight with Iron Tongue had been subtle, on deep levels. The sensation he experienced now was as subtle as a hammer-blow to the head. "Claybore attacks," he whispered.

"To the battlements. I knew he planned an attack soon, but thought it would come after he took Bron."

A flash of insight told Lan that Claybore had already been victorious over Jacy Noratumi's city—and what of Inyx?

He raced after Wurnna's ruler, found a circular staircase up, and took the steps three at a time. He emerged on the city's defense wall, peering down the long canyon. Only a few of the grey-clad soldiers peeked out around the bend from their camp.

"*Die!*" bellowed Iron Tongue. And Lan watched the few curious souls perish at the command. But the magical pressure did not lessen—it mounted higher and higher every second.

"Claybore commands this attack," he told Iron Tongue. "I know it."

Iron Tongue paid him no attention. The ruler-mage turned and faced his city, crying, "To me! All mages to me!" The power of that command caused Lan to take three quick steps toward Iron Tongue. He backed off, awed at the power exerted. If that iron organ in the man's mouth had once resided in Claybore's mouth, Lan knew the power it had given. If Claybore regained it, he would be invincible. The simplest of words became an unstoppable command. Coupled with the potent spells Claybore knew, entire worlds could be toppled from their orbits, continents razed, kingdoms conquered.

"We meet again, dear Lan," came soft words. Lan smiled as Rugga stood beside him. He noticed she kept her distance from Iron Tongue. Whatever existed between ruler and woman had to be stifled until the attack had been repulsed.

"Use the power stone," commanded Iron Tongue. "Draw on the power to form a spear point aimed at Claybore's throat!"

Lan almost fainted at the intensity of the surge rising from within Wurnna. The fifty-two assembled sorcerers coordinated their spells perfectly. Lan had little chance to examine this phenomenon—it had something to do with the tongue resting in their ruler's mouth. He joined in, adding his power to the magical thrust at Claybore. While the spear was a magical construct, it took on physical reality. Lan studied and learned, even as he lent his own strength to hurling the weapon.

The thrust missed. A swift riposte was deflected by Iron Tongue's powerful spell, but Lan felt the magics slithering away, not stopped, but merely redirected. In Wurnna hundreds died.

The air came alive with writhing creatures of the innermost imagination. They were dispelled. Returning went sharp jabs, subtle prods, anything Iron Tongue could launch against Claybore. But each parry and magical riposte carried a penalty. Lan felt Rugga weakening. He wondered at this and then saw fully half of Wurnna's mages were dead or dying. Claybore took a frightful toll.

And Lan hadn't even noticed!

Lan moved closer to Iron Tongue, keeping his arm around Rugga's waist. She resisted weakly, then allowed him to drag her along. It soon became obvious she was unable to contribute significantly to the battle. She had

been drained of all energy, even though tapping into the
power stone surrounding them. With great reluctance,
Lan allowed her to sink to her knees on the stone
battlements.

The conflict intensified. How, he couldn't say.
Wurnna's number diminished steadily, yet their lightning thrusts grew in power. Once, Iron Tongue looked
at him, a quizzical expression on the man's face. Lan
ignored it. He became engrossed in finding new magics,
producing different spells to hurl at Claybore.

Then came the words he dreaded to hear.

"Defense! Form a defensive barrier!"

Iron Tongue turned away from attack to simply protecting what remained of his Wurnna.

"You can't," Lan screamed. "Claybore will destroy
us all."

But he was alone. Iron Tongue and the handful remaining wove a solid wall of energy that crackled and
shimmered. Nearby, they exerted more power and stopped
Claybore's attack. Lan reached down and gripped Rugga's
limp hand. She tried to squeeze his fingers, but the
strength wasn't in her.

Angered, Lan Martak bellowed, "You shall not win
so easily, Claybore! Not this time!"

The anger boiled and surged and fed upon itself.
Fleeting memory of what Iron Tongue had magically
forged rose in his mind. Those were spells he had never
seen before, but they were now his—and more than his.
They took on a writhing, sensuous life of their own,
horrible in its awareness, horrible in its stark hunger for
human life.

Dragons of purest ebon space formed. Lan Martak
unleashed his creatures to suck at Claybore's troops.
The canyon widened under their ravenous feeding, rock
and earth and humans vanishing. Claybore exploded
them, one by one. By then Lan had formed new spells,
ones he did not comprehend.

All around him, space and time churned and boiled away. Eerie silence fell. Light faded and sensation died. All that remained was Lan Martak standing on a stony abutment and the fleshless skull with sunken eye sockets blazing forth ruby beams.

Lan and Claybore fought to the death in a magical realm beyond reality.

CHAPTER TEN

"You cannot win. You will die." The words reverberated through Lan Martak's skull to the point of pain. He blinked back tears of searing acid and stared straight into Claybore's ruby-glowing eye holes. In past encounters, he had somehow managed to avert those deadly beams, forcing them away harmlessly. As curious as anything, he sought their deadly virulence and faced them fully.

And absorbed their death. And returned it tenfold to Claybore.

The dismembered mage twitched as the reflected beams struck his fleshless skull. The magics intensified. Spells became more complex, more intricate, more life-threatening. The land about the duel-locked pair quaked under the intensity of their battle. Lan Martak took all Claybore had to offer and gave it back with a power and an expertise he had never before possessed.

"The youngling has learned much, I see," came Claybore's words, words not formed by flesh-and-blood lips. They echoed through Lan's entire body; he *had* learned. In some fashion those words were weapons. Instinctively, he robbed them of their edge.

"I have. Give up your quest, Claybore. Retire to a

world. Stop enslaving those you encounter along the Road."

"You have learned much magic but nothing of my nature. I will never stop until I am again whole. Terrill robbed me of my arms and legs, my flesh, my every organ." The torso, supported on magically powered mechanical legs, twisted about, allowing Claybore to break eye contact with his adversary. "I am the aggrieved. I seek only that which was—is!—mine."

Lan felt no need to debate the point. Claybore's goal might have been acceptable. What intelligent being could exist as a mere skull in a box? Only his motives and methods were questionable. The young sorcerer began weaving new and more deadly spells, ones he barely understood, ones so potent none dare commit them to paper for the incautious to find. From somewhere beyond reality came the dancing mote that now gave information. Reading the surface of that twinkling speck allowed him to probe Claybore's weaknesses.

And the dismembered mage had weaknesses. Lan's surprise at learning this almost caused him to drop his guard. Claybore had seemed so powerful before, so dominant in all situations. Now, in a confrontation, his power seemed almost pathetically small.

Lan Martak reconsidered. It wasn't Claybore's power diminishing, it was his own prowess increasing. He had come a vast distance in ability from sensing magics and being able to work petty fire spells.

His ebon dragons sucked life out of the grey-clad soldiers, but did nothing against Claybore. Vultures with wings of fire formed above Wurnna, spat out their cries of rage, and launched themselves in fury at the renegade sorcerer. Only last-minute shiftings of his defenses allowed Claybore to disperse them and their beaks of the coldest steel.

"Materializations? Where did you find that conjuration?"

Lan had no answer.

"The mages in that pitiful little city cannot help you. You are alone, worm. Grovel before my might!"

The attack Claybore launched forced Lan to his knees. Needles of burning agony drove into his body from every direction. No nerve, no muscle escaped the mind-stunning misery. Focusing on the mote within allowed Lan to fight the pain scourging his body; he did not stop the anguish, but could ignore it. The surface of the luminous mote rippled and boiled, turning into itself and revealing texture and substance he'd never before noticed. And feeding its pseudo-life came power from the very bedrock of Wurnna.

In the distance, he heard hushed tones muttering, "He uses the power stone."

The power stone. The rock mined in the valley of spiders. It did more than provide heatless light. It fed his magics, gave them scope and range unlike anything he had imagined before.

Slowly, muscles protesting, Lan struggled to his feet. He countered every thrust Claybore made. The pain faded until only its haunting memory lingered. But Lan couldn't renew his attack.

He and Claybore were deadlocked.

Then a new element entered the conflict. Quiet, subtle, Iron Tongue began speaking.

"You are a mighty sorcerer, Claybore. One of the best. But even you can show mercy. Now. You show the spirit of brotherhood so well known among all mages."

Lan realized the words meant nothing. Carried along with their seductive cadence came a magic that was irresistible. His battle with Claybore had weakened the mage adequately for Iron Tongue's sorcerous suasions to work. A hesitation came to Claybore's attacks. They lessened, even as Lan weakened under the onslaught.

"I will allow you to consider surrender, worm," came the mage's words.

"Surrender is not the answer," Iron Tongue insinuated softly. The words carried no volume, no command, but the effect became increasingly dramatic.

"We . . . we will meet again. I will triumph!" In the distance Lan saw the fleshless jaw clacking. Mechanical arms and legs waved about, then carried Claybore away, as if into a dense fog. Soon only a dull glow from the heart-sphere locked into the armless and legless torso remained; then it, too, vanished.

Lan sank forward, hands resting on the cool stone battlement in front of him. Sweat poured in vast rivers across his face, into his eyes, under his arms and even down his legs. He controlled the trembling.

"You saved me," he told Iron Tongue. "Your magic worked on him. He gave up when he might have conquered."

"You held him," Iron Tongue said, his words oddly accented. "Such power as he commanded this day all of Wurnna could not turn away. You did it with no help. You will stay and aid us in our continued fight." The words softened, became lilting and seductive. "Wurnna has much to offer. We are friends. We can give you all you need. You are one of us. And there is Rugga, lovely, loving Rugga."

Lan Martak recognized the spell being woven about him by Iron Tongue's words, but lacked the strength to fight it. Or did he? Even after the life-and-death struggle with Claybore, he felt more vibrantly alive than ever before. The young mage straightened and allowed his thoughts to lightly brush the surface of the brilliant mote dancing so deep inside him.

"Do not attempt to ensorcel me, Iron Tongue. Your chants are potent, but the wrong way of winning my further assistance." Lan bent and helped Rugga to her feet. The woman's face was as white as flour and she had a wild, half-crazed expression. She had touched magics far beyond her abilities. Lan sent his mote dancing through her mind, burning and probing, touching and healing. In minutes, she shook as if she had a palsy, then collapsed.

"Get her to her chambers. She will sleep off this ordeal."

The expression on Iron Tongue's at this feat of healing assured Lan that, even in a city of sorcerers, his powers had grown drastically and far outstripped the others—with the possible exception of Iron Tongue himself.

"Fully a thousand greys were destroyed by the dark dragons," came the report. Lan swallowed and found his mouth dry. He had slaughtered a thousand men and women with a single spell—and it had required no more effort than lifting a spoon to his mouth.

He pushed his still-filled plate away. He had eaten voraciously, but the death toll took the edge off his hunger more than the food had. The young mage did not enjoy the power growing within him, yet he had to learn to control it and use it against Claybore. Things had been so much simpler when he had hunted the forests, loved Zarella, and had never heard of Claybore or his grey-clad legions.

"Why me?" he wondered aloud.

"Lan? You said something?" Rugga sat beside him, her warm thigh pressed intimately against his under the table. Her hands had strayed many times during the meal, but he had tried to ignore the urgings.

Lan had become cautious of the woman's attentions. Ever since entering Wurnna, he more clearly noticed motives in others. Hers hinged on more than simple lust for him. He shook his head. It took no mage to understand what Rugga wanted. The power struggle between her and Iron Tongue for control of the city was a thing of the past—because of Iron Tongue's histrionic abilities. Any new element entering the game gave Rugga another chance at seizing power.

Power. It always revolved around control over others.

And Lan Martak was learning to play for his own ends.

"Such a lovely necklace," he said softly. Even softer he added, "And such a lovely neck."

"Only the neck?" she teased.

"And the face. And the regions . . . lower." He allowed his eyes to drink appreciatively of the woman's lean beauty. As he did so, Lan realized that some portion of that beauty was magically enhanced. Rugga cast minor spells to soften her somewhat masculine angularity and enhance what was already present. At some other time in his life, Lan would not have minded, if he had even noticed. Now it angered him. Rather than assume she did it for his enjoyment, he decided she wanted to bind him through her body.

"All yours, my Lan. Let us go."

"Not yet," he said, glancing down the table at Iron Tongue. The mage sat back in his chair, arms crossed over his chest, eyes dark and clouded with suspicion. Lan had to defuse that suspicion enough to make use of it without fanning it into outright opposition.

"These dinners always become so insufferably stuffy. *He* never allows anything interesting. Like I offer."

"Rugga, my lovely, in a moment. First, tell me of that necklace. It appeals to me." The sensations racing up his arm as probing fingers lifted the baubles from silken skin seemed so tantalizingly familiar, yet he failed to put a name to them. Iron Tongue supplied it for him.

"Those are polished power stone. They are used for decoration as well as utility. After it is taken from the ground, I energize it with spells known only to the ruler." Lan knew Iron Tongue idly boasted; the spells to activate the stone seemed quite simple to him, now. But Lan knew that Iron Tongue talked for a reason other than conveying information.

The words boomed forth, resonantly touching the deepest parts of Lan's being. He wondered if Iron Tongue did it on purpose, whether he controlled the magical organ in his mouth fully. If Iron Tongue allowed anger to intrude, he might prove a more dangerous opponent than even Claybore. Lan couldn't forget the way Iron Tongue had persuaded Claybore to break off the attack when the other mage had had victory within his grasp. The tongue was a potent weapon, indeed, and one which would make Claybore invincible if he recovered it.

"How did you come to discover the stone?"

"We of Wurnna have always known of it. The mines close at hand petered out."

"And required you to begin mining in the valley of the spiders," Lan finished.

"Just so. By the time we began mining there, we were dependent on the stone to energize our entire civilization. A few of my magical spells is all it takes to provide limitless power from the rock."

"It multiplies your magics?" Lan frowned. He *felt* it did more than this, but couldn't say exactly what else.

"Somewhat. My particular use—and it differs for every mage—is to add to my personal force." Iron Tongue held up an arm entirely braceleted in the power stone. The jewelry rippled and danced with coruscating, many-faceted gems. "I draw on their power. With Rugga, she uses them to enhance her beauty." The words carried an insult. When Rugga stiffened, Lan reached under the table and seized a wrist, holding her down, soothing her with his presence. She subsided;

Iron Tongue obviously counted this a minor victory in their power struggles.

"I feel more when near the gems," said Lan.

"Each mage draws slightly different powers from them. This is another reason we use slaves to mine the ore."

They didn't trust any single sorcerer to be near such a vast vein of the power stone. Wurnna lived in turmoil, both internally and externally, Lan surmised.

"Can't you come to some accord with Bron and the spiders? You don't need to enslave when you can get them to aid you in return for the objects that only you of Wurnna can offer."

"Why barter when we can take?" snapped Iron Tongue. "They have no sorcerers in their rank. Inferior. They are our inferiors. And the spiders are mere animals."

"Intelligent animals."

"You speak well of them, Lan," said Rugga. "Have you forgotten they tried to feed you to their odious hatchlings?"

Lan said nothing about one of his friends being an arachnid. Nor did he mention Inyx or her trip to Bron. Instead, he replied, "Claybore divides you. You fight Bron and they fight back. You battle the spiders and they eat your slaves. It wouldn't surprise me if Bron and the spiders were also at war. And you all fight Claybore." He shook his head sadly. It was no wonder that Claybore and his legions had conquered most of this world so easily. The spiders posed no threat to the marauding sorcerer; Claybore had claimed that Bron had fallen; only the organ resting in Iron Tongue's mouth remained for Claybore's victory on this planet to be complete.

"We could have eliminated the others long ago. It amuses me to allow them to remain." Iron Tongue sounded diffident, but Lan read the real reason behind the claims. Wurnna depended on Bron for workers and the city's rulers maintained the spiders' threat as a method of control. Without some menace, Iron Tongue might not remain at the forefront of the city, even with his potent abilities.

Lan changed the course of the conversation abruptly, asking, "How did you come by Claybore's tongue?"

Iron Tongue stiffened.

"He's had it for over a decade. His father died and willed it to him. It is the symbol of power for our city-state." Rugga sounded bitter as she told this to Lan. The young mage didn't have to be told she'd have willingly cut out her own tongue for a chance at the power that the organ afforded her ruler.

"The origin of the tongue is lost in myth," said Iron Tongue. "One of my forefathers forged it magically and has handed it down through the generations."

"It belonged to Claybore," Lan said, more to test reaction than to inform. Rugga looked at him curiously, as if he had struck his head and wasn't quite sane. She believed in the mythic origins cited by Iron Tongue. But Iron Tongue's face clouded over with anger; he knew that Lan spoke the truth.

Without a word, Iron Tongue rose and stalked from the room. Other mages hovering around the perimeter of the room talked among themselves in hushed tones, occasionally pointing and sending small, harmless questing spells in his direction. Lan let out a pent-up lungful of air and shoved himself back in his chair. The legs scraped on the power-stone flooring in the room.

"Rugga, my lovely," he said, "show me how the power stone renews strength after strenuous activity."

She smiled wickedly and rose, holding out her hand for him to take. They left, aware of the stares of those in the room. Lan knew he played a dangerous game aligning himself with Rugga, but internal policy in Wurnna interested him far less than triumphing over

Claybore. Only by incurring Iron Tongue's anger did he see a way of winning the worlds-spanning struggle with the dismembered sorcerer.

But Rugga showed him that certain of those steps could be enjoyable. Very enjoyable.

CHAPTER ELEVEN

"We can't outrun them," Inyx gasped. "They close on us, no matter how we confuse the trail."

"This is my country. They will not find us." Jacy Noratumi sounded more confident than he felt. The soldiers had proved more tenacious than he'd thought. When he and the other pathetic few had fought their way through the defensive wall of what remained of once-proud Bron, he had thought to simply walk away, that Claybore would be content with conquering the city.

Leaving his home to the grey-clads had rankled more than anything else in his life. He felt he had given up too easily, yet he saw that Inyx was right in her advice to abandon the city. To carry on the fight, he had to be free to roam, to chevy, to retaliate in whatever fashion came to his fine brain. Dying with his city was a noble gesture, but one which denied Noratumi's true duty to its citizens.

Revenge now drove him, and Inyx figured prominently in it.

"There are too many of them. I . . . I think they use seeking magics on us. Lan told me of his home world where they use sniffer-snakes, magically enhanced creatures to smell out prey. They are almost impossible to elude or defeat.''

"These are flesh-and-blood soldiers following us," Noratumi said flatly. "As such, they can be killed with a good sword thrust." He demonstrated by slashing at the air above his mount's head. The animal whinnied and glared back at its rider as if to protest such cavalier behavior.

"We can't run from them forever. They will wear us down. We need time to establish a base."

The man knew Inyx was right. Without at least a week to find and establish a secure camp in the mountains, they would be ineffective and kept on the run. Sooner or later they would falter and the grey legions would have them at their mercy. From Claybore, Noratumi expected no mercy at all.

"We can double back and try to regain the city, then. Bron is vulnerable. Claybore would hardly expect such an attack."

"The reason he wouldn't expect it," Inyx said bitterly, "is that it'd never succeed. We need an army. Look. Do you see an army?"

"I see nobility in these refugees. They will fight, if I so order."

"They'll fight and die, then," snapped Inyx. "Twenty—fewer!—are not enough to lay seige to a city. With Claybore's mages conjuring constantly, they could wipe us out without endangering the hair on a single soldier's head."

"Why doesn't he use this vaunted magic to stop us now?"

Chills caused Inyx to shiver in spite of the sun's warmth on her back. She spent much of her time glancing over her shoulder, certain that the grey-clads had ridden them down.

"He doesn't need to expend the energy. The soldiers can follow. But I suspect a mage accompanies them to

help track us. We have used tricks designed to slow
the finest of hunters. None has worked. Can you explain that, if not through the use of magic?''

Jacy Noratumi sullenly shrugged, turning away from
the dark-haired woman. He had never met one like her
before; she fascinated him with her independence and
quick thinking. That she swung a sword better than
most of his citizens only added to his admiration of her.
He just wished she'd stop harping on this Lan Martak.
He'd met the man briefly at the oasis and had seen little
in him to justify such loyalty.

Noratumi couldn't bring himself to believe Inyx actually loved Martak—a mage and a spider-lover! What
perversity!

"We must find a base. Soon." When Noratumi didn't
answer, Inyx pressed on, this time voicing what she had
hoped he would intuitively understand. "We must make
our peace with Wurnna. They can offer the sanctuary
we require."

"Wurnna? Never! Those demons would enslave us.
Sooner would I throw myself on my sword than even
attempt to ally with them."

"Bron and Wurnna have warred long enough. Bron
is no more. They can use our aid to save Wurnna.
Claybore no longer has to divide his forces. He can
bring the full force of his army against Wurnna now. If
you want to preserve this world for its native inhabitants—
for yourself—this is the only way."

"Better Claybore than Wurnna ruling."

"You can't mean that." Inyx saw Noratumi's resolve weakening. She softened her approach, rode closer
and reached out to place her hand on the man's shoulder.
"Claybore will never be satisfied with less than total
obliteration. His goals do not require anyone living on
this planet. He must be stopped. Soon."

"But Wurnna," whined Noratumi. "They are Bron's

sworn enemies. For centuries we have fought one another.''

Inyx didn't need Lan's magical powers to understand the nature of the struggle. They fought one another; they also needed one another. The external threat hardened resolve and allowed cohesion of culture and purpose that wouldn't have existed otherwise. If either had triumphed, that would have required new territories to be explored and exploited and conquered. Both Bron and Wurnna had enjoyed and profited from the local conflict. With Bron no longer in the matrix, Wurnna's rulers faced what had been, until recently, unthinkable. They fought a foe capable of actually destroying them.

"Give me another idea."

Silently, Jacy Noratumi reined toward the notch in the mountains leading to Wurnna. The sag of his shoulders told of his lack of enthusiasm for the journey. At times being a leader carried burdens too intense for any man.

"The refugees come," said Iron Tongue.

Lan nodded. He, too, had sensed their approach through the tortuous mountain trails. Since Rugga had gifted him with both a bracelet and necklace of the power stone, he found it easier to use his magical abilities. Casting spells, minor and major, no longer tired him as it once had. He marveled at the powers he had accumulated and now exercised; the power stone freed him from physical exhaustion. His magics opened vistas into the universe that dazzled him. At times he felt exultation rivaling any god's and at others he became humbled at the task ahead of him. These powers weren't for his personal use. In some way he didn't yet understand, Lan Martak traced back the source of the magic to his home world. The Resident of the Pit had touched him and caused the burgeoning of latent magical powers within his breast.

Duty and pleasure. Those magics provided both. He had to use them for betterment along the Cenotaph Road—and that meant countering the evil Claybore had wrought.

"Jacy Noratumi is with them," he said. Lan didn't mention Inyx's accompanying the small band. The less Iron Tongue knew of his personal life, the less power the ruler of Wurnna had over him.

"Bron is lost. I shall enjoy seeing Noratumi sweating in the power-stone mines. He has taunted me in the past. Now I shall laugh."

"We need them—and not in the mines. How many were killed during Claybore's last attack?"

"No mages."

"No mages," agreed Lan, "but fully half the population of Wurnna perished."

"Slaves. A few citizens."

"Many," insisted Lan. "You need even a paltry handful of refugees to swell your ranks. Defending the city requires men and women acting because they want to and not because they fear being enslaved."

"We will talk with them," came the soothing words. Iron Tongue used the full power of his tongue. Lan paled slightly, then countered the effective magics with deadening spells of his own before he agreed with Wurnna's ruler.

"Noratumi wants us to meet them outside the walls," Lan said.

"How do you know this?" demanded Iron Tongue.

Lan didn't answer. That he had received this communication from Inyx came as revelation and relief for him. His new powers showed him that they wouldn't have to be apart again. While distance might separate their bodies, their minds could remain in contact. The flow was blurred and indistinct now, but he knew it would grow with practice. He wanted it to grow. He needed the dark-haired warrior woman more than he had thought possible.

A small hand signal from Lan stopped Inyx a dozen paces away. She flashed him a puzzled look, then studied Iron Tongue. Understanding slowly dawned on the woman. This was the man Claybore sought; this was the man with the magical tongue; this was the source of the misery and suffering on this planet.

"Iron Tongue," said Jacy Noratumi without preamble. "I seek asylum for my people."

"Only thirteen of them." A sneer twisted Iron Tongue's lips. "The mighty ruler of Bron governs only refugees." He laughed cruelly and the sound echoed off the mountains and and rumbled down the canyon toward the spot where Claybore's troops had once made their camp. Only death remained there or beyond, where Lan's ebony dragons had devoured human flesh.

"You do little better," snapped Noratumi. "Wurnna crumbles bit by bit. How many of your citizens are left?"

Iron Tongue started to lie, then tempered it when he saw the expression on Lan's face.

"Enough to survive."

"Inyx claims we can unite against Claybore."

Iron Tongue turned his attention to Inyx. The woman returned his bold stare without flinching, even though something curled and writhed deep within her. Iron Tongue was a man of infinite cruelty. His very gaze threatened to strip away her humanity. When he spoke, he humbled her. She wanted to fall to her knees and worship him.

Only Lan's level tones pulled her out of the spell cast. Her vivid blue eyes widened as she grasped the full importance of both name and power possessed by Iron Tongue.

"She is my friend," said Lan, glad that Rugga had

remained behind in Wurnna. Still, Iron Tongue would make certain this datum got into the other woman's hands. He played political games constantly, jockeying for advantage—it wasn't enough to possess supreme rhetorical skills in a city of mages.

"So? She is welcome in Wurnna." Iron Tongue smiled insincerely as he said, "and so are our brothers and sisters from fallen Bron."

"For them, I accept," said Noratumi. "For myself, however, I prefer to stay outside the walls of your city."

"Jacy, we need you. We need your talents. You are the tactician we need," pleaded Inyx, gripping his sleeve and tugging slightly. He never looked at her.

"I will not enter that city. Not while *he* rules it."

Lan and Inyx exchanged looks. The nonverbal link between them formed but their confused thinking prevented any but general emotion from flowing. Inyx inclined her head slightly, indicating she desired a private conference. Lan nodded. While it wasn't vital that Noratumi close ranks with his mortal enemy, it suited Lan's own plans if he did so.

Plot. Counterplot. He was beginning to conspire with the best. He and Inyx walked away a few feet to talk.

For what must have been a minute, neither spoke. They were content simply staring at one another. Lan reached out and tentatively touched Inyx's cheek, almost afraid she might be an illusion sent by Claybore to torment him. If she were a wraith, Claybore outdid himself. The cheek flushed under his touch and turned warm. Strong fingers gripped his wrist and pulled him closer, her red lips coming to his. Eyes flashing with desire, she started to kiss him.

"Wait," said Lan. "This isn't the time. Once we are in the city, then we can speak."

"Speak?" she mocked. "Is that all you want to do? It's been an eternity since we saw one another."

The silent communication that had been sparked now flared into a full two-way flow of information. Along with it came emotion undeniable to the woman of what Lan Martak felt for her.

"Lan my darling, I shouldn't tease you like that. I . . . I know how you feel about me."

He swallowed hard and held her close when a tickling sensation started at the borders of his mind. Claybore launched a new attack.

"We must get inside Wurnna's walls soon. The power stone helps protect us."

"What of their mages?"

"Most are dead. Most of the ordinary citizens—and slaves—are dead, also. I found in your mind the last moments of Bron. Are these the only survivors?" He indicated the haggard band of refugees resting in their saddles.

"As far as I know, these are the only ones to escape. They had no way of deflecting the magics Claybore hurled at them. If Wurnna had been more sympathetic, there might still be two outposts against Claybore."

"How do we persuade Noratumi to join forces with Iron Tongue?"

Inyx shook her head and said, "I see no way. He fears, and legitimately, that Iron Tongue will enslave him. The truce might cover the common survivors of Bron, but never a leader. Jacy is wary of all sorcerers, you included, Lan."

"I suspect there is more to it than that," he said dryly.

She looked at him sharply, but said nothing. Inyx almost blushed, something she had not done since before her marriage to Reinhardt. The bits and pieces of information she had read in Lan's mind corresponded to those he had gotten from hers. She did not know if she was prepared for such intimacy. Of body, yes, but of mind? That was a step beyond any she had taken.

"What will we do? I sense Claybore's attack is close."

"You feel it, through me? Interesting." Lan's mind took in the datum and continued on, constructing various schemes and discarding them as he went. "I must talk with both Noratumi and Iron Tongue. They will either agree or cut one another's throats by the time I am finished."

He and Inyx rejoined the others, upper arms brushing as they walked. Lan rejoiced in the woman's nearness. They had been apart far too long. The brief sojourns with Rugga had counted only as political dealings in his mind, just as Inyx's dalliances with Jacy Noratumi fell into the same category. He almost smiled to himself. He had outgrown petty jealousy, the jealousy that had precipitated his departure from his homeworld when one of the grey-clads had murdered his lover. But was this newfound maturity worthwhile? He had come to think in terms of temporary alliances, what was to be gained from the politics of the flesh.

Lan decided it was. His love for Inyx only deepened. And, if the brief rush through her mind was any indication, the soft emotion was shared.

"Noratumi, Iron Tongue," he said. He motioned for the two leaders to join him. With small twitchings of his fingers, he wove a spell that dulled Iron Tongue's persuasive powers. He found it impossible, as yet, to completely negate the tongue's enhancements, but he didn't need that at the moment.

"I have decided. I will never set foot inside those walls." Noratumi's words fell monotone, determined.

"What makes you think you would be welcome?" said Iron Tongue. "Your people are needed. You? Ha! You are a worthless leader who lost your city-state. What else but failure can you bring to Wurnna?"

"All our skills are needed," Lan said patiently. He tried to analyze why Iron Tongue's words carried such magic. In dim ways he began to understand and use a weaker version of the spell. "Wurnna needs the numbers. Noratumi's people need a new home."

"Only until Bron can be rebuilt."

"That requires Claybore's defeat. Work for it, Jacy. With Iron Tongue."

"I will not be a slave in his power-stone mines."

"Who'd want a lazy snake like you? It wouldn't be worth the whip leather to beat you."

The two leaders glared at one another. Lan cut through the mounting hatred.

"A truce. Temporary, until Claybore is routed. Iron Tongue, do you agree not to enslave Jacy?"

"Only if he works in the mines of his own free will. Without the stone, we cannot triumph. You know that. You came to the same conclusion."

"Will you, Jacy, work freely in the power-stone mines if it means victory?"

"Yes, but you are promising something that will never be delivered, Martak. The spiders prevent easy access to the mines. Even with my people, we are too few to fight *and* mine."

"If I grant free access to the mines, will that satisfy you both?"

"A treaty with the spiders?" scoffed Iron Tongue. "Impossible."

"Will you agree to all we've talked about, if I can do it?" Lan wrenched the reluctant nods from both men. He heaved a deep sigh and indicated the narrow dirt path leading back into the safety offered by Wurnna. The magical pressures mounting indicated Claybore forged another massive offensive. He needed the vast reserves of power stone within the city to feed his own defenses.

Juggernauts of prodigious power—all illusory—smashed

against Wurnna's defenses for twenty solid hours. By
the time Lan, Iron Tongue, and the remaining sorcerers
had reached the point of exhaustion, so had Claybore.
The offensive slowed and finally vanished.

"How long, Lan?"

"I don't know," the young mage told Inyx. "Claybore
might start up again at any minute. He is almost as
powerful as all of us within the walls. The power stone
is all that feeds our defenses now."

"Can't you use that little grimoire of yours to find a
new spell that will stop him?" She pointed to the brown
leather, brass-studded book Lan had dropped on a nearby
table. He had been given the book of spells by a dying
mage atop Mount Tartanius.

"I've looked. Some of the spells come easily now. I
used several to send the black dragons into Claybore's
soldiers—and I hadn't even remembered seeing them
until Iron Tongue and the others worked with a modi-
fied version. I changed the spell slightly another time,
but Claybore now counters it easily. There's so much I
don't know!" He came to the point of frustration-caused
tears. He had come so far, yet the path stretched to
infinity before him. Claybore had spent centuries learning his magics. Lan Martak was a newcomer to this
form of battle. He had unwillingly entered an arena
where a strong arm and a quick sword meant nothing.

"Try to relax. Don't force yourself to the brink of
exhaustion."

"And you have just the remedy for that, I take it?"

"Of course I do."

Her lips crushed into his even as her hands wandered
along his muscular body. For a moment tiredness seized
him and he almost told her to stop, then he drew down
and found almost limitless strength in the bracelet of
power stone he wore. The change from lethargy to
vitality took Inyx by surprise, but it was a nice surprise.

Her fingers laced through his brown hair and he rolled over and between her inviting legs. The expression on her face as he began the ages-old rhythm added to his energy more than any magic locked within a power stone. They merged and became one in body and soul, using their newly found rapport, soaring, exploring new and exciting realms that finally exploded in a wildly satisfying finale.

Long after Inyx had slipped off into sleep, Lan lay beside the woman, his arms about her gently breathing form. When he fell asleep, the dreams he had feared came. Once more Claybore invaded his innermost thoughts and brought evil visions.

Laughing, the fleshless skull of the dismembered sorcerer taunted him. When Lan Martak awoke in the morning, he had slept but not rested. He had witnessed what Claybore plotted all night long.

CHAPTER TWELVE

"I see no reason to go on this ridiculous journey. You will fail. I know it." Iron Tongue stood with arms crossed tightly and a quizzical expression on his face. Lan Martak had felt the full magical force of the man's persuasions and had turned them aside like a rich man ignoring the beggings of some street mendicant. Never had a human withstood the awesome power of the tongue resting in his mouth when he had turned it against him—before now.

"I shall not fail. To show good faith to the spiders, the leaders of the groups involved must be in attendance." Lan didn't add that he wanted them with him to keep from sundering the fragile truce. While it was dangerous concentrating all resistance leadership in one small party away from the safety of Wurnna, Lan had decided that the risk of the alliance failing was greater. He wanted to be close to soothe ruffled egos and tend what might be a full-time job of working negotiated apologies acceptable to all when slights, both real and imagined, occurred.

If they could not persuade the spiders to allow open mining of the power stone, Wurnna was doomed. If they simply remained within the walls of the city-state,

Claybore's attacks would eventually wear them down. The potential for success was greater by taking this desperate gamble.

"He will sense us. Claybore is inhumanly endowed."

"He isn't endowed at all," said Inyx. "Not physically, at least." She glanced at Lan and smirked.

"I referred to his sorcerous powers. I am fully aware of his bodily dismantling by Terrill," said Iron Tongue. Lan scowled at this. Iron Tongue was quick to cite the mythic origins of the tongue he used, yet he claimed to know about Terrill and the gargantuan struggle across worlds that had resulted in Claybore's dismemberment.

"I can get us past his soldiers. There are small spells that he won't bother to check for," Lan responded.

"Small ones are all you can summon," Noratumi said bitterly. "Otherwise, you would end this battle here and now."

Lan ignored the jibe. His reunion with Inyx hadn't been well-received in any quarter of the city. Jacy Noratumi resented him; so did Rugga. He had seen the pair together early this morning, dour expressions and impassioned gestures highlighting their meeting. That made him smile. He had maneuvered them together to discuss their mutual problems and to find that Iron Tongue presented a common barrier to understanding between Wurrna sorcerers and Bron miners. Politics depended mostly on "chance" occurrences being engineered in such a way that the used did not realize it. But an eventual alliance agreed on between Noratumi and Rugga mattered little to him at the moment; a supply of power stone counted for more. Lan didn't know if an ample supply of it improved their chances or not, but he wasn't going to attempt a frontal assault on Claybore without it.

"We leave in one hour." He didn't wait for the protests. Let them cry on each other's shoulders. That might forge a stronger bond than anything else he could do.

"Sentries," Inyx said quietly, pointing with the tip of her sword. Lan's fingers moved restlessly in an effort to create the proper spell. He strove to achieve not invisibility, which was a potent enough magic to draw Claybore's attention, but non-noticeability such as that used by Rugga on their journey into Wurnna. If properly cast, the sentries would see them but their eyes would report no danger to their brains. Their passing might be reported but it might also be ignored as inconsequential.

"I do not like this," said Jacy Noratumi. "Let's kill them and make sure they do not report us."

"Silence," snapped Iron Tongue. "The man is creating a delicate spell."

Whether Lan's concentration flagged for a moment or some other element entered the arena, none can say. The nearest guard noticed them. Even as his frown wrinkled with the effort of recognizing them, Inyx acted. With a perfect *fleche,* she took four quick steps forward and skewered him. The guard's death, however, shocked the others into action.

"Escapees! Kill them!" cried the sergeant of the guard from his post higher up on the side of the mountain. Frustration at garrison duty, fights against insubstantial and totally deadly dragons and other illusory beasts, and the deaths of his fellows all powered the attack.

Lan started to conjure up the spell that would bathe the grey-clads in flame. He held back at the last possible instant. Such magic would definitely draw Claybore's attention. Unsheathing his sword, Lan waited for the soldiers to attack. The blade felt odd in his hand; only now did the young mage realize how he had come to depend on his spells. Before he had learned so much, the sword and he had been as one, flowing and thrusting, moving and parrying and lunging.

He again fell into this rhythm of attack, skewering the first soldier to confront him. At his side, Inyx slashed powerfully to sever a wrist. The grey-clad gasped and stared numbly at the spurting stump. Turning pasty white, he pirouetted and slowly sank to his knees, more dead than alive.

"Ha! This is more like it!" came Noratumi's happy shout. The sounds of metal ringing against metal filled the small draw. Pent-up frustration at the destruction of his city boiled over and caused the man to fight like a small platoon.

Lan's muscles protested at first, then relaxed as he became used to the movement of his sword. Having Inyx at his side aided him more than he could put into words. A quick disengage drove his point into an exposed throat. The next man tried fancy footwork; an unexpected replacement carried Lan's tip to its target in the man's heart.

Even as he fought, he sensed magics building. He turned to warn Iron Tongue, trusting Inyx to protect his flank.

"No magic," he cautioned, but the ruler of Wurnna had already spoken the soft words.

Lan dropped his sword as he fought against the spell conjured by Iron Tongue. He robbed it of all its power— but in time? Was Claybore alert enough to have detected the leakings of such magical power?

Iron Tongue snorted in disgust, then used his voice.

His Voice, Lan mentally corrected. When Iron Tongue spoke, all listened.

"Cease fighting." The greys obeyed, confusion running riot in their expressions. They had been in full battle. Why stop? Their enemy bled and died. They outnumbered them ten to one. Victory was within their grasp! They stopped.

"Have them drop their weapons and forget this even happened," Lan said.

Iron Tongue laughed harshly. His words did not reflect what Lan had asked for.

"Fall on your sword points." One after another of the soldiers impaled himself on his sword. In less than a minute, all lay dead by their own hand.

"That wasn't what I wanted," Lan raged.

"Perhaps not," said Noratumi, "but for once I side with the sorcerer. I only wish I had such power. All those scum would die by their own blade, if I could do such magic."

"More guards on the way," Inyx said softly. "The trail up the cliff's face is all that's open to us. Unless we return to Wurnna."

Lan glanced up the treacherous path. He hadn't intended for them to traverse this narrow, rocky, exposed route, but there could be no retreat now. He sheathed his bloodied sword, vowing to clean it later; then he started up the trail without a backward look. Let them follow or not. He had a mission to accomplish.

Lan Martak sat on the rounded boulder and stared down into the valley of spiders. The path to this point hadn't been as dangerous as their start had suggested it might be, but it had been no summer idyll, either. They had avoided a half-dozen patrols and killed only three more of Claybore's soldiers. How long it would take for news of those deaths to get back to the dismembered mage, Lan couldn't guess. The pressure of time mounted on him, however. Holding Iron Tongue and Noratumi together was a problem, but holding the spiders' Webmaster and the other two as well posed an almost insurmountable task.

And that was just the beginning. After the treaty came dangerous mining operations continuously vulnerable to Claybore. Lan would have to launch an attack to distract the sorcerer from the power-stone mines; that meant a major battle he wasn't sure he was up to waging.

"First things first," he said under his breath. A hand rested on his shoulder, squeezed comfortingly. His hand covered Inyx's to acknowledge her support.

"Can you do it?" she asked.

"I'm counting on Iron Tongue's histrionic powers to sway the spiders," he admitted. "If that fails . . ." He shrugged. Planning everything to the most minute detail wasn't possible. The best he could do now was to try, then change tactics if the situation demanded it.

"They've spotted us. An efficient warning system." Inyx pointed to the webs strung across the mouth of the canyon, webs that had been added since Lan's escape.

Lan heaved himself to his feet and said, "Stay here with the others. I'll try to get the Webmaster's attention for a parley."

"No. We all go."

He started to object, then nodded. What she said made sense. Give the opening parley the best shot possible. If they failed, no amount of talk would have sufficed. Allowing the spiders to eliminate them one at a time struck him as ridiculous now.

Together, the four humans marched down until they stood under the swaying web across the valley mouth. Lan swallowed and tried to force spit into his cottony mouth. While a single spell on his part could destroy all the spiders, he dared not use it. Not only did it go against his principles to wantonly destroy so many intelligent beings, such a spell would bring down Claybore on them.

"We desire an audience with Webmaster Murrk," he called out to the black speck high above in the web. The spot darkened, became larger. The arachnid dropped like a stone from space.

"Lan!" Inyx drew her sword, her fingers nervously drumming on the hilt.

"Careful," he said. "Do nothing to anger them."

"It doesn't matter. Look! They're going to eat us!"

Lan hated to admit that Jacy Noratumi could be so right. Other spiders dropped from the web, their intent clear. One swung in a long arc past them, mandibles clacking ferociously. Noratumi thrust, only to have the steel blade severed by a spiderish snap.

"Iron Tongue," he called. "Speak to them. Tell them to stop."

"It'll do no good. I have tried persuasion on them before. They don't—or can't—listen."

"Try it, damn you. We can't fight them."

"A pretty fix you've got us into," complained Noratumi, throwing aside his broken sword and pulling out a small dirk. He fought to the death, no matter how ludicrous it seemed to fight such overwhelming forces.

"We come under the banner of truce," said Iron Tongue. The words caused shivers to pass up and down Lan's spine. He heard the words and he *believed*. Everything Iron Tongue said now, he knew was the absolute truth. "Do not harm us. We come in peace to negotiate."

Iron Tongue heaved a disgusted sigh.

"See? They pay me no heed. Spiders, ha!"

"No spells. Not yet," said Lan, menace in his voice. While he lacked the sting of authority Iron Tongue possessed by virtue of the oral organ taken from Claybore, he had learned much about commands. Iron Tongue allowed a burgeoning spell to die on his lips.

Lan faced the one spider on the ground, sword sheathed. "We mean no harm. We want to speak with Murrk."

The mountain arachnid advanced, a flesh-and-blood killing machine bent on destruction.

"Oh, do stop this silly posturing, Kingo. I am ever so positive Webmaster Murrk desires to speak with them.'' The voice came from the aerial walkway. Lan recognized it immediately.

"Krek! You're still alive!''

"Of course I am, you silly human. I am much too valuable to the web for them to eat me or chase me out. I have been attempting to reason with Murrk. Your presence at this time is most fortunate. I believe he is slowly coming to see there is another way of dealing with you humans, other than devouring you, that is.''

"That's Krek,'' said Inyx, slumping forward and gripping Lan's arm. "And am I ever glad to see him.''

"And I you, friend Inyx. Now please wait until I contact the Webmaster and arrange for a proper meeting. Whatever you do, do not disgrace me with your impetuous ill manners.''

"Anything you say, Krek, anything you say.''

Both Iron Tongue and Noratumi scowled at Lan. They hadn't considered him having an ally in the spiders' camp.

"No fire spells. I will grant you that much of a concession.'' Iron Tongue stood with arms crossed, a glum expression on his face. Lan Martak sensed how closely the man held himself in check, wanting to rage out and destroy Murrk. The giant spider hung upside down from a web strand; his expression was unreadable by any human.

"That is as much as we might expect from you deceitful humans. My good friend Krek assures me that one of you is honest. Which one, I cannot say since you all look alike.''

"While they are lacking in the proper number of legs, that one is my friend and ally.'' Krek poked a leg in Lan's general direction. "And that one,'' he continued, indicating Inyx, "is also of a noble bent. More so than the other, I do believe. In fact—''

"Krek, never mind the lengthy explanations. Murrk wants to be sure Iron Tongue won't use the fire spells against your webs. I guarantee that he won't."

"Very well, friend Lan Martak." Krek rubbed legs together and let out a shrill screeching noise as he spoke with the Webmaster. Murrk bobbed on his strand but said nothing else.

"There won't be any trouble mining the power stone?" asked Jacy Noratumi. "We're not doing this for our health, you know."

"I thought that was the, *only* reason," Iron Tongue said haughtily.

"We get paid for this."

"Paid? Isn't your continued futile survival worth the risk?"

"Lords, wait," said Lan, intervening before the two came to blows. To Noratumi he said, "The way is clear, assured by our alliance with Webmaster Murrk. You and your crews can mine the stones and transport it unhindered."

"We take all the risk, even with the spiders docile," complained Noratumi. "He sits on his fat ass inside Wurnna's walls. He waits for the power stone all snug and safe."

"There are risks all around. Claybore must be kept occupied or he'll attack the mines. We need that ore. Iron Tongue will maintain Wurnna's defenses and launch occasional forays to divert Claybore's more magical attentions."

"He can't enslave any of us anymore. Not ever, after we're clear of the greys."

"Iron Tongue? That sounds like a fair deal to me. No more slavery. Noratumi's people will be risking their very lives for you." Lan saw this argument made little impact on Iron Tongue. The mage had slipped over the thin edge of sanity once more; the glazed eyes and exultant expression worried Lan.

"They are doomed. Haven't they shown their inadequacy by losing their own city? But very well, those who survive this will be forever free citizens," Iron Tongue replied.

"And our children and their children," Noratumi continued.

"Do be serious. Wurnna *needs* workers. I'm willing to allow a handful of you to run about as if you were free citizens, but let's not carry this to ridiculous lengths." The man's voice changed in timbre. Lan's fingers wove a complicated pattern in the air to defuse the effects of Iron Tongue's honeyed words. When the mage saw that his usual persuasiveness wasn't working, the man finally agreed with ill grace.

"They cannot shoot at us while we hang in the webs," said Murrk. He indicated Noratumi and the bow he carried.

"They won't. If they do, they answer to me personally." Lan felt a wave of relief as all decided this was as good a deal as could be worked. They parted to separate camps, Noratumi to one side of the ravine and Iron Tongue to the other. Above moved Murrk, on his way to more mundane administrative duties.

Krek, Inyx, and Lan remained in the sandy spit. Inyx was the first to break the silence.

"This isn't going to work. Someone is going to get mad and start the war up again."

"I hate to admit it, but you're right," said Lan. "About the only thing we've got working for us is that the power stone will have to be mined quickly. Maybe we'll get it back to Wurnna before some hothead breaks the alliance."

"Maybe all the Lower Places will frost over and the demons wear fur parkas," Inyx mumbled.

"Stranger things have happened around Lan Martak," observed Krek. Both humans glared at him and went to soothe whatever injured vanities the meeting had created.

• • •

"Claybore attacks more quickly each time after retreating," said Lan, a distant look on his face. "Iron Tongue is holding him back quite well, however. Purely defensive. It won't be long before Claybore begins to wonder why we don't launch an attack since that's the only way to ever win free of Wurnna's walls."

"The mining is going well enough," said Inyx. "Jacy's crew opened the old shaft in less than an hour and found a rich vein of the power stone. It amazes me how quickly they work."

"Fear," said Lan. "They're driven by fear of the spiders dangling above them as if they're waiting to pounce."

"Why should a friendly spider engender such a response?" asked Krek. "We mountain arachnids are peaceable enough creatures, unless riled."

"Peaceable? You're bloodthirsty, amoral, and totally without conscience," said Inyx, laughing.

"Why, thank you, friend Inyx. One does try, but it is so difficult at times to live up to the high ideals of one's culture."

Lan had long since given up trying to fathom the contradictions in the spider's brain. Sometimes gentle, other times a veritable death machine, Krek ran the gamut of responses to what appeared to Lan the identical situations. To Krek, however, those battles or retreats carried different moral values. About all Lan could be certain of was Krek's undying friendship. The two had been through a great deal together and had come to depend on one another.

Even then, there were times. . . .

"Martak!" came the call from the mine. "A word with you."

Lan went to see what bothered Noratumi.

"We've got enough of the rock loaded onto the

wagons for Iron Tongue. With this much he can move the moons out of the sky.''

The three wagons visibly sagged under their load. The power stone left a cloud of dust hanging about that wouldn't dissipate, even in a moderate breeze.

"Let's start moving it out. Time is vital. Iron Tongue holds back Claybore's assaults by a hair's breadth.''

"Not so fast. I've been thinking. About them.'' The man pointed to one of the spiders hanging a hundred feet above. "I might have misjudged the bugs.''

"They're gaining freedom from intrusion. The privacy of their web is important, as is their safety. For all their size, they are fragile enough beings.''

Noratumi waved that away with a nervous gesture. "I want to give them something more. For not bothering us.''

"What?''

"In the mine we found some cave mites. I know the spiders eat them but don't like going after them. Well, we thought we might drag some out for the spiders.''

"I'll ask.'' Lan turned and quickly conversed with Krek. He saw his friend's dun-colored eyes glow with the news of the cave mites. The young mage didn't need Krek's animated bobbing agreement to know the arachnids would be happy to feast on the mites.

Whatever Lan had expected, he didn't expect to see the eighty pound eyeless larvae that Noratumi and the other miners dragged forth from the bowels of the shaft. The sickly white creatures thrashed weakly, visibly dying from the weak rays of the mid-morning sun. They weren't allowed to suffer long; Murrk and the others descended from their webs and began devouring the mites.

"Messy,'' said Noratumi with some distaste, "but I suppose they think the same about the way we eat.''

"How long before we can reach the trail leading into Wurnna?'' asked Lan, more important things on his mind. The effort required to sneak in such a large quantity appeared to him insurmountable, but Iron Tongue had assured him and Noratumi that Claybore would never find this path—and that he'd be otherwise occupied when they brought their load in.

"Weeks," came the answer. "The loads are too heavy for us to haul, except one wagon at a time."

"Can't do it that way. One time we might get through Claybore's troops. He'll be alert for a second try." Lan toyed with an idea, then pushed it aside. Using magic would only draw Claybore's attention. But wasn't the risk they all took equally as great by not employing certain spells?

"What are you thinking, Lan?" Inyx sidled up to him, her arm pressing close.

Excited, he said, "I haven't had a chance to look through the grimoire, but one spell sticks in my mind. I haven't dared try it before. There hasn't been the time—or the need. Noratumi's miners can't get the wagons up the steep roads. They aren't strong enough to do the pushing, and the horses are hardly better off. But a demon turning at the axle could give enough torque to make it possible."

"A demon?" Inyx warmed to the idea. "Yes, one like I found in Dicca. The one turning the rotor on that fluttercraft. It was tiny, but so stong!"

"I'll need to conjure at least three of them. Holding them bound for a short while might be possible. It just might be." Lan wandered off, deep in thought. Inyx went to talk with Jacy. The two argued but the miner eventually agreed as Lan wandered back, a broad smile crossing his face. "I know exactly how to do it. It . . . it seems so simple."

"Then do it. The spiders seem sated for the moment, but I have no wish to press my luck." Noratumi tilted his head in the direction of Murrk and several other spiders. Lan had to agree. The alliance worked well at this instant. But the next?

He went to the nearest wagon and crouched by the rear axle, examining it. Running his hand over the work-worn wooden rod sent shivers of anticipation into his body. This was the first chance he had to consciously think about his conjuring before doing it. The black, eerie, empty dragons he had sent against Claybore had come without the slightest thought on his part. But this required effort.

Lan closed his eyes and let the dancing mote deep within him rise up. It bobbed and darted about, grew closer, took on texture. He teased it with his mind, captivated it with chants, bound it with his magic. The almost-alive ball of energy swung to and fro, then vanished from his inner sight. In the span of a heartbeat, it returned, herding a tiny demon with massive arms and wrists. The demon screamed its protests, but the mote suffocated all words.

Silently, Lan pointed. Fire leaked from his fingertips; the demon understood. With a sour expression, the diminutive horror from the Lower Places jumped up to sit, legs swinging, from the axle. It bent its head to keep from bumping against the loaded wagon bed.

The young mage made a turning motion with his hands. The demon squawked loudly enough to be heard over the damping spell cast by the light mote.

"Master, give me a break! That is not possible. My arms will tire. My hands cannot grip without slipping. There'll be blisters. I'll hurt myself! I have a hernia!"

"Do it," Lan said coldly.

"Oh, all right. I'll try. But if this doesn't work like you think it ought to, don't say I didn't tell you so." The demon bent double and wrenched at the axle. The entire wagon creaked and groaned and began to slowly move uphill, even with the brake firmly in place.

"Noratumi, get the team a'pulling. I've bound a

demon to the back wheels to give you a boost up the hills. Be careful going downhill. The creature is likely to keep twisting.'' Lan glanced under the wagon and saw that the demon had intended doing just such mischief. Thwarted, it had to think up other misdeeds. Capturing a demon was relatively simple; binding it to exactly his will was another matter.

As soon as Noratumi began the wagon on its trip back to Wurnna, Lan summoned another and still another demon. The last one appeared different. The first two had been purple with distinct red tints in the piglike eyes. Not so this one. Bright green, its eyes glowed a baleful amber that reminded Lan of the mechanicals he had encountered on other worlds. This creature was totally supernatural—but its nature troubled him. Not only did the beast not complain at its imprisonment, it willingly began working, doing twice the work of the other captive demons.

''Inyx,'' Lan said in a low voice, ''be especially watchful of the last wagon. The demon works too hard.''

''Without urging? That *is* something to worry over.'' She remembered her own brief encounters with motive power demons. All had complained bitterly, begging for release from cruel masters, and all were more than anxious to be slackers at their work.

Lan Martak trudged along with Inyx and Krek, scouting ahead and guarding the flanks as the caravan of wagons lumbered through the mountain passes. The spiders watched them leave their valley without so much as a wave of a hairy leg. Lan fancied that he recognized Webmaster Murrk high in the webs, but Krek informed him he was mistaken.

All day they rattled and rolled along a rocky path scarcely the width of the wagons. Only at the end of the second day did Lan begin to think there might be a chance for success. The secret passageway Iron Tongue had promised turned out to be a tunnel drilled directly through the mountain to the west of Wurnna. Lan sent his energy mote ahead scouting for any sign of Claybore or his troopers. The route remained clear of both physical and magical impediments.

The third wagon rattled into the narrow passage, following the other two. Lan and Inyx brought up the rear.

"We're so close. I have a premonition of disaster."

"Precognition?" the woman asked.

"Nothing so firm. Just an uneasy feeling. The trip from the mine has been too easy."

"Too easy?" Inyx flared. "We fought for every inch. Even with your demons, getting those tons of power stone ore up the mountains was anything but easy."

"I meant that Claybore hasn't bothered us. With Bron obliterated, he has troops to spare. He can comb these mountains. If he wants. Why hasn't there even been a small magical probe?"

"The battle might have drained him more than we thought."

Lan Martak didn't believe that for an instant. With his newfound energies, he also gained insight into Claybore's powers. The sorcerer did not share mortals' weaknesses. He had different flaws; tiring easily was not one of them. Like Lan, he drew on powers transcending the ordinary.

"The gap opens!" came the echoing cry from the far end of the tunnel. "We're almost there. Wurnna is in sight!"

"Now comes the hard part," Lan said. Barely had the words left his mouth when the green demon on the last wagon let out a grunt of supreme exertion.

"Lan?" Inyx wasn't sure what was happening. The mage knew instantly and began strengthening his binding spells. But the damage had been done. The demon had exerted its full power to send its wagon rocketing ahead. The heavy ore wagon ran over its lead horses, crushing them with wild whinnies of pain, then picked up speed on a slight downhill stretch and smashed full-bore into the second wagon.

The tunnel filled with power stone and choking clouds of dust. All within the tunnel would suffocate before reaching the safety of Wurnńa.

CHAPTER THIRTEEN

"A full frontal assault. That will do it," the woman said with finality. Alberto Silvain looked at his companion and started to speak, then thought better of it. Kiska k'Adesina had changed during the course of the siege of Wurnna. The half-crazed glare in her eyes had intensified to become that of a person totally insane. Silvain had tried to reason with her on finer points of military tactics, to no avail. She had Martak and his spider trapped within the city—all she cared about was her revenge.

"That will not do it," came Claybore's emotionless voice. The officers turned to see mechanical legs scissoring back and forth to bring the torso and head into their map room. The eye sockets in the fleshless skull glowed a cherry red. Silvain straightened, anticipating a sudden lance of death. None came.

He relaxed slightly. This battle did not go as he anticipated and he did not want Claybore blaming him. To shift the accusations of culpability he needed a lever. His opportunity might come soon with Kiska less and less able to reason rationally.

"Master, your will is all," cried a now docile k'Adesina. The wildness remained in her eyes but it was tempered with . . . what? Silvain tried to understand what went on in the woman's mind. That brain was a capable one. He had firsthand evidence of it in her planning for the conquest of Bron, but other things fluttered and distracted her, things not reasonable or even sensible.

"Of course it is," snapped the skull, jaws clacking in a mockery of human speech. "I have just annihilated one of their parties as they tried to sneak into Wurnna." The words came slower, more carefully chosen. Silvain's attention perked up. The dismembered sorcerer did not tell all. Who had been destroyed? Martak? The spider? Would Claybore be openly boastful if he had eliminated those two major impediments to his regaining his body?

Silvain decided that, had Claybore been victorious over the young mage, he would never mention it in front of Kiska k'Adesina. He knew of her psychopathic need for personally killing the man and monster who had slain her husband. To blunt such a valuable instrument as k'Adesina was out of the question.

Alberto Silvain relaxed even more. If this truly meant Martak and Krek were dead, that made the defeat of Wurnna all the more certain. Martak had been far too lucky in their brief encounters; whom the gods favored with such luck, they tended to be enamored of. Silvain played it as safe as possible in dealings of this magnitude. Crossing the gods was as unthinkable as spitting on the skull grotesquely propped up on the armless and legless torso.

"No frontal assault," declared Claybore. "Now. Give me the plan that will succeed."

Silvain started to speak, to cover for his companion, but the woman raced into a full battle plan that had to be contrived on the spot. And for all its hurried and incomplete qualities, Silvain again marveled at k'Adesina's genius.

"The flanks are weak. We gain the heights of the

mountains and fire down upon them. A few troops will be enough. The canyon leading to the front gates of Wurnna is protected by Iron-Tongue's magics. Down that corridor must go an attack based on sorcery.''

''Yes, I quite agree,'' said Claybore. ''Since that devil Martak used the ebon dragons and fire vultures, I have been reconsidering my own role.''

''Can you conjure creatures to rival those?''

''Of course I can,'' Claybore said irritably. The depths of those limitless eye sockets began to pulsate with ruby light. ''There are spells to counter such minor illusions. I plan something more. Yes, something vastly more imaginative and deadly.''

''Patriccan and his minions can add their feeble powers to yours, master,'' said Kiska. ''Every spell, no matter how tiny, can aid us in this great endeavor.''

Silvain felt a momentary giddiness. How alike k'Adesina and Claybore were. Both improvised on the spot and both were geniuses, twisted and lacking totally in conscience. His position in such company became more precarious by the instant, but he had no other choice but to remain to the end. His world devastated by Claybore's power, he had to cast his lot with the sorcerer or die. It had been rewarding enough, as long as he didn't think about the death and destruction he ordered. In a way, it was only retribution.

His world had been killed. Why not kill others?

''Silvain,'' came Claybore's cold words. ''What do you contribute to this scheme?''

''Master, you have summed up the finer points so well, only small details remain to be worked out.''

''Such as?''

''The troops commanding the mountain slopes and looking down into Wurnna must be equipped with some weapon capable of diverting attention. Something magical, perhaps? On my last world, we used fire elementals to power aerial machines. When they fought, they opened ducts, allowing the elemental's flame to flare forth. Such a minor application might even bring about Wurnna's capitulation.''

''You want the troops to command fire elementals?''

''Command? No, master, but something as potent will be required if they are to be taken seriously.'' Silvain sensed the sorcerer's instant antagonism toward such magics being used by common troops—or even by Kiska's captive mage, Patriccan.

''Equip those troops with catapults. I will prepare pots of stone burning fire. Will *that* occupy those in the city?''

''Master, you will be invincible.''

Silvain looked at Kiska and made a tiny motion with his head, showing displeasure with her ready acceptance. He cleared his throat, working to phrase his thoughts properly, so as not to offend Claybore.

''Master, such would work, but the effort required getting such assault engines up the cliffs might take weeks. May I suggest that you authorize Patriccan to use magics to shove boulders off the mountaintops? This requires little effort after gaining the heights.''

''I want Iron Tongue. I want what rests in his mouth. It is mine! All else is . . . is mere game. Get that tongue and your reward shall be immense. Fail and you shall rue the day. Do what is necessary.''

''We will not fail!'' cried Kiska k'Adesina.

''The magics you have authorized will overwhelm the remnants of Wurnna, Master.'' Silvain bowed low as the mechanical carried Claybore from the room. On the floor where the mech had stood pooled oil from a leaking joint.

Silvain stared at the empty doorway for some time, then turned back to the charts, pointing out vantage points for k'Adesina's approval. While part of his mind worked on the details of conquest, a larger portion worried over the irrational feeling that this battle would be his last.

"The troops are ready. They will not fail us." Kiska k'Adesina proudly surveyed the assembled rows of soldiers. Silvain eyed them with less than optimistic eyes. The troops appeared beaten, having spent too long in the field, been under fire too often. The dragons that had roared and devoured both officer and enlisted alike sapped courage sorely needed for a real offensive against Wurnna. Convincing even the field officers that victory would be theirs became increasingly difficult. The battle would have to be joined soon or the entire force would fall apart under its own fear.

"You have done well," Silvain lied. He idly wondered why he bothered with these games. There was little conviction in aiding Claybore in his goal. All Alberto Silvain could say was that Claybore still appeared the most likely to be victorious—and Silvain always bet on the side of the strong.

"Thank you," Kiska said, her eyes blazing with demonic light. She clutched at his sleeve and pulled him toward her. The needs she conveyed so primitively almost overwhelmed the man. A musky smell hinted at the woman's level of desire. Silvain wondered if this came from imminent battle or something else.

He smiled, his lips curling upward slightly. It was the power k'Adesina worshipped, the need for revenge driving her to it. But which was means and which was ends? They mingled in a heady brew for the mousy-haired woman.

"Come, let our officers attend to the final preparations. We must confer. In my quarters." Silvain pitched his voice low. Before battle it always relaxed him to find a willing woman. With Kiska k'Adesina, he had one more than willing. She was a panther springing on her prey.

Barely had he entered the canvas flap to his tent when she swarmed over him, bearing him down, smothering him with her barbaric affections. Revulsion flared and died in a split second. Silvain needed this contact as badly as the woman. What matter that she was as crazy as a wobblebug? Top command in Claybore's force offered few chances for pleasure.

Silvain took his now, k'Adesina giving as she took.

Passion locked them for a long time as their crotches met and ground together, their bodies strained and sweated, their pulses pounded like drums in their foreheads. Their desire abated slightly, then built to a fever pitch once more. Neither held back. Raw, naked lust boiled forth as they completed their coupling.

"We will find Martak and I shall have his ears first. Then I will pluck out his eyes. No, no, those I save. Next I'll flay him alive. *Then* out come his eyes." The woman cackled, over the edge of insanity once more.

Silvain pushed her away, sitting up and searching for his grey uniform. He wished she hadn't spoken those words so closely on the climax to their sexual acrobatics. His agile mind now worked on what had been going through her head as they made love. He didn't like the possible routes her fantasies might have taken as he drove himself deep within her yielding flesh.

"Claybore will require our presence for last-minute details," he said, his needs sated. Calmer now than he had been in some time, inner pressures resolved, Alberto Silvain became again the perfect soldier with no doubts or hesitation about what he must do in the hours to come.

"Claybore. Yes, yes, you are right." The naked woman leaped out of the rude bed and began drawing on her uniform. In other circumstances Silvain might have found the sight of the creamy flesh erotically enticing. Now he felt—nothing. It was as if all emotion had been drained from his body and mind. Step springy and soul dead, he sought out his master.

Claybore twitched slightly. The mechanical carrying his torso and skull obediently bent forward at the hips in a completely inhuman display of flexibility. A wire-driven arm lifted and cogwheels ground together in a noisy clatter to move charts off a large wooden table. With care more appropriate for carrying a babe in arms, the metal fingers closed on a tiny clay tablet and moved it to the edge of the table.

"Careful, fool," snapped Claybore. The mechanical continued to move the tablet to the spot ordered by the master sorcerer. "There. There is where I desire it." The metallic fingers opened and left the tablet propped up slightly so that the empty eye holes in the skull might peer down on the flat clay surface.

Light churned and blazed in the pits of those eye sockets. Red, blue, then green light erupted to bathe the inanimate clay slate. For long minutes nothing happened, then the slate took on an eerie glow that radiated from deep within. It shook slightly with a vibrant power that manifested itself as deep humming sounds.

A picture formed on the featureless tablet.

"Ah, there it is. The product of my dealings with the demon. Lan Martak, you fool, to think you could oppose me. All you have done is delay me, irritate me, make me angry!" The last words rose in a crescendo of hatred. The full spectrum of the rainbow blazed in the mage's eye sockets. Claybore calmed himself to study the scene.

The tunnel opened near the walls of Wurnna. It was here that Martak had thought it possible to sneak back into the walled city with three loads of the power stone ore. Claybore chuckled to himself. Martak was such a fool. He had never learned that nothing went unobserved in the realm of magic. Every spell, no matter how minor, caused "ripples" to form on the fabric of the universe. Those sensitive enough to the "ripples" might trace them back to their source.

Claybore had known from the start about the mission to the valley of spiders, of Noratumi's miners and the three demons summoned to help power the heavy ore carts up the steep mountain roads. He had known all and sent one of his allies. The green demon had done well. While the dust from the power stone cloaked even this magical vision, Claybore saw the havoc wrought.

Men and women lay crushed and ripped apart like so many marionettes with their strings clipped. The two lead wagons had wrecked, and he was sure that the third one plugged the tunnel. In that tunnel would be the dead bodies of Martak and Inyx and the meddling spider, suffocated from the choking dust.

"A fitting end. They thought to defeat me with that power stone. Instead, I turned it against them!" The sorcerer gloated for only a few more seconds. He had other uses for his all-seeing eye.

The scene shifted rapidly to a vantage high above his own camp. Spiraling downward with gut-twisting speed, he focused just inside the roof of Silvain's tent. There he witnessed his two top commanders passionately locked in the rictus of sex. If he had the power to so move his skull, the mage would have nodded. This worked better and better for him. Let their human frailties bind them more closely to one another—and to him.

Silvain's role would become clearer as the day wore on. Let him grab what frail pleasures he could.

He had hesitated in telling k'Adesina of Martak's death. Hatred drove her, made her a better officer, gave her the reckless abandon in the field he would require to regain his tongue from that usurper in Wurnna. She held sway over Patriccan, and that sorcerer would be needed for the final assault. Claybore needed k'Adesina's allegiance. He would not inform her of Martak's demise.

While Claybore thought that Alberto Silvain guessed that Lan Martak and the others had perished, to him it meant little. Promise him nothing more than hydraulic release of his passion and he would remain quiet.

For Claybore it was all so simple. Use one against the other. Toy with their emotions and bind them the closer.

"Now," he said aloud, the word ringing through the emptiness, "now is the time. We attack. And soon I will be able to speak—and to utter all the power spells now denied me!"

The slate hardened, the picture vanished. As the mechanical bearing Claybore's body turned to leave, the magically spent tablet crumbled into grey ash.

CHAPTER FOURTEEN

The green demon squawked as it worked to spin the rear axle faster and faster. Lan Martak's first reaction was to grab, to physically hold back the runaway ore wagon. Then common sense and his newfound powers took over. No man, no matter how strong, could possibly slow that load. Instead, Lan reached down within himself and teased the dancing mote to life. The point of brilliance had become his guide, his companion, his source of power in realms he had yet to fully explore.

The savagery of the situation instantaneously communicated to the light mote. It blazed with indignant power, then flashed off, out of Lan's line of sight.

Its response came too late. The crazed green demon smashed its wagon into the rear of the second one. The power stone surged up and out of the wagon, its momentum barely checked by the collision. The resulting roar almost deafened those in the tunnel. But that was the least of their worries.

"The dust. I can't breathe," cried Inyx. She choked and gasped as billowing dust raced toward them from the wrecked wagons.

Lan knew full well that suffocation would be a merciful death compared to what might happen if they too

169

deeply inhaled the power stone dust. His mote of light had failed to stop the demon's suicidal mission, but it now served in a completely different fashion. Like a membrane drawn over a drumhead, the light diffused and formed a curtain between Lan, Inyx, and Krek and the source of the danger.

"It'll be all right. Just hold your breath for a couple seconds." He looked at the way the curtain of palely shimmering light held back the dust and fragments of stone flying at speeds faster than he could track. The way the ore reacted reminded him of corn tossed into a campfire. Tiny explosions recurred at random, sending pieces hurtling outward. Every time one of the power stone shards hit his magical curtain, it exploded into actinic brilliance.

"How long will that continue, friend Lan Martak?"

"I don't know," the young mage admitted. "But we're safe as long as the shield is in place."

"Safe? How can you say that? There are men and women on the other side dying because you used some damned demon who double-crossed you!" Inyx raged, but he knew it wasn't directed at him personally. She hated the idea of being unable to help the others trapped in the raging maelstrom of power stone.

"While I do share friend Inyx's concern about the others," said Krek, "she and you both miss an important point. Claybore knew of our excursion. He senses magics just as you do. Even one of little or no training, as you are, is capable of detecting a spell in use."

"He can't 'see' us now, no matter how good he is," said Lan. "The power stone is setting up some sort of continuous reaction. The magics are all jumbled. The energy locked within the raw ore is prodigious. With it we could have easily defeated Claybore. Now, it only serves to shield my own magic use."

"Then turn your spells against Claybore." Inyx stood defiantly. Dust coated her face and turned her into a chalk statue. Krek stood to one side in the narrow tunnel, shaking and brushing one leg against another in a vain attempt to remove the same dust.

"If I could, I would. But he remains too strong. Our best course is to go on out of the tunnel, see if we can salvage any of the power stone, and get inside Wurrna's walls as quickly as possible. Let Iron Tongue activate it and then we can attack Claybore."

"Perhaps this is a suitable opportunity to use your power against Claybore," suggested Krek, "but in a more restrained fashion."

"What do you mean?"

"Spy on his camp. Learn of his troop preparations. We spiders care little about such things, but you humans value such oddments of information. Though why, I cannot say." Krek sank down, legs curled about him, hardly more than a dark lump in the narrow tunnel.

Lan didn't bother answering. He split off a portion of the shield blocking out the power stone dust and sent it streaking through the nonworld it inhabited and into the air above Claybore's camp. Through this aerial porthole he witnessed the grey-clads moving to mount their attack. Lan lacked control over the sky-spy, but what he saw chilled him. The troops marched with more determination than he'd have believed after his dragons had grazed among their ranks. Claybore—or k'Adesina or Silvain—had instilled a battle fever that would carry them to their deaths on Wurrna's battlements.

The brief glimpse of an exposed chart carried in the hand of an officer made Lan shake his head. The canyon walls on either side of Wurrna would soon be scaled and the heights occupied. None but a sorcerer might use those heights to advantage, but Claybore and his mage-assistants knew enough spells to destroy Wurrna, given the chance.

"We must rejoin Noratumi and the others," he said. Inyx's head came up and her eyes gleamed strangely.

Lan felt a pang of jealousy. What had gone on between her and the Bron leader? Then he pushed it from his mind. He had no time for petty emotion. This was a day of bold moves—and bloody deaths.

The curtain of light pushed away from him as he advanced. The faster Lan walked, the quicker the seal moved. It passed over the wrecked wagons but all power stone and dust was shoved before the light curtain. When daylight shone down on his head, Lan relaxed and allowed the curtain to coalesce once again into the mote he had come to depend on.

Dust billowed upward and roiled about, obscuring bodies and crushed wagons, but Lan and his friends stood in a small clearing in the atmospheric confusion.

"Jacy!" cried Inyx. She repeated the name until a battered, bloodied figure stumbled through the dust and waved to them.

"I never thought I'd see any of you again. Iron Tongue abandoned us. Went on into Wurnna. It . . . it's all over. I feel it." Jacy Noratumi sank to his knees, more unconscious than alert.

Lan closed his eyes and chanted a simple healing spell. Noratumi gasped and fought for breath. Lan ignored his plight and Inyx's pleas for him to stop. Only when he had magically plucked the last of the dust from the man's lungs did he allow breathing to resume normally.

Noratumi fell forward, supporting himself on hands and knees. He turned dazed eyes upward to Lan and said, "I can feel the change within me. What did you do?"

"You are whole again. I must heal the others before the power stone dust kills them. The death is not a pleasant one."

Noratumi made a mask out of his tunic and rushed back into the perpetual storm of dust boiling about the entrance to the tunnel. In a few minutes he led back a small band of survivors—too small. Only four still lived.

Lan Martak found the healing both tedious and simple. He drew on the power of the dust itself to bring about the cure, yet he chafed at the delay. He needed these four; he needed a thousand times their number. Magics alone would not win this day's battle.

"We must hurry. Krek, go into Wurnna and tell Iron Tongue to get crews out here to salvage the power stone."

"He returns even now," the spider said.

Lan forced a small tube of clarity through the obscuring dust and saw a wagon recklessly driven across the short distance between postern gate and tunnel mouth. Seated beside the driver was Iron Tongue. His lips moved in a slow chant. Lan guessed he goaded the driver to even more suicidal daring in reaching the wrecked wagons.

"Begone!" came Iron Tongue's loud command. The spell carried enough power and authority to dissipate the dust cloud in seconds.

"Why didn't you do that?" demanded Noratumi.

"He's had more experience with both power stone and spell," said Lan, but the words sounded lame to him. All the more so when he saw Inyx's expression. He went to greet Iron Tongue.

"Don't take a second longer than necessary," said Iron Tongue. "Claybore's attack is already launched. We *need* this ore. Badly. Now!" He used the full power of his tongue to goad the humans into frenzied action.

They all fell to loading the ore onto the good wagon that Iron Tongue had brought back from his city. When only half a load had been accumulated, Iron Tongue clapped his hands together and ordered, "Into the wagon, all! We must retreat. The attack is upon us!"

Even as he spoke arrows came arching downward to

embed themselves in the ground at their feet. Lan casually brushed them aside with a quick spell of only minor potency; his attention focused on the heights on either side of Wurnna.

"Iron Tongue, how do you defend those areas?" He pointed out the spots that worried him most.

"Defend them? Why bother? Nothing can reach us inside the city from there."

"Claybore's magics can. He has a clear view of everything within Wurnna from either canyon wall."

"We have always picked off any enemy attempting to scale those cliffs. We will again. Our archers are good. Come, Martak, worry over important things. Can we activate enough of this power stone for our projectiles?"

Lan frowned. He hadn't known Iron Tongue wanted the ore to place in rockets. He had assumed the rock's use would be to aid mages in countering Claybore's magics and in powering offensive spells. Quick fingers brushed over the bracelet of the power stone given him by Rugga. To waste all the power stone by shooting it at Claybore's troops seemed ineffectual—and it made their sacrifices to this point trivial.

He maintained the magical dome over them to ward off arrows, but he "felt" something else building, something of a diabolically magic intensity.

"Claybore hides his troops with invisibility spells. They . . . they are so apparent to me now." Lan's voice conveyed the shock he felt. Only a few weeks before, the idea of detecting any complex spell would have seemed a miracle to him. Now he analyzed and located the nexus for spells he only barely recognized. "There. He sends his troops up the mountains, just as I warned."

He and Krek exchanged looks. They remembered all too well how Kiska k'Adesina had followed them into the foothills around Mount Tartanius on a far distant world. The woman had been raised in mountains, knew their dangers and uses in war intimately, and could fight ferociously using their rocky strongpoints.

Their wagon crashed and bumped along until the gates of Wurnna slammed behind them. They had ridden around, ignoring the small postern gate in favor of a larger one that accommodated their laden wagon. Even as the driver slowed and applied the brake, workers rushed forth to unload the pitiful amounts of power stone salvaged from the three wrecked wagons.

"To the battlements. From there I will launch my messengers of death. Claybore will go to his death mourning the day he attacked Iron Tongue and Wurnna!"

"Claybore is immortal," said Inyx in a small voice. "Even the great Terrill couldn't kill him."

"The heat of battle goes to his head," said Noratumi. "He is overconfident. He doesn't realize Claybore's true power."

Lan said nothing. He had a different idea and it didn't sit well with him. The tongue resting in Iron Tongue's mouth was once Claybore's. Did some measure of that sorcerer's evil personality carry over with the organ? Or was Claybore able to reach out and subtly influence Iron Tongue into foolish recklessness? Whatever the answer, the result would be the same.

"The heights will soon belong to the greys," said Rugga. Her concern for Jacy Noratumi drew Lan's attention as much as the woman's words. "We cannot use the rockets on them. There won't be enough. Even working full speed, we cannot convert more than a fraction of the ore into the explosive and propellant needed."

"Get to the battlements. Help him as you can," Lan said to Rugga and Noratumi. "We might find luck on our side, at least for a short while."

"What do you mean?"

"When I looked down into his camp, I saw preparation for a massive assault. If Claybore uses only a physical attack, we might buy some little time. Not much, but enough.''

"Enough for what?" Inyx sounded bitter. Lan wondered if it was due to their predicament or the way Noratumi responded to Rugga. He had not been able to find the time to explain to Inyx how such a friendship strengthened their chances for victory. Inyx still responded to Jacy on a personal—intimate—level that was now a thing of the past.

"We aren't able to hold him at bay indefinitely. Without the power stone, Claybore will swarm over us and end it all quickly—unless we receive outside aid.''

"From where? Bron is only a dim memory. The other city-states have long since surrendered. Only the—'' The dark-maned woman's eyes widened in disbelief. "Lan, you can't be serious.''

He nodded glumly.

"The spiders might be all that's left for us.''

"Murrk will never aid humans. He is well content with the treaty worked between us.'' Krek swayed to and fro in a dizzying motion. The spider's agitation did little to bolster Lan's idea of possible help from the valley.

"It might not be necessary. Let's see how Iron Tongue's rockets work.''

Even as they climbed the battlements, Lan focused on the rocky crags jutting on the east and west flanks of the city state. The canyon that had provided the defense was being turned against them now.

On the walkway, Iron Tongue chortled and rubbed his hands together.

"This will do them just fine. Launch!''

Lan turned and shielded Inyx from the back flare of the erupting missile. Its tail ignited and lashed backward with the pent-up power of a released fire elemental. For a long instant, it hung suspended, then overcame inertia and blasted forth to arc up and come down amid the front ranks of Claybore's advancing army. The explosion was as blinding as the launch.

"There. That'll show them."

"They still march on us," came Rugga's tired voice. "It will take more to stop them this time. Much more."

"The rockets will do it." Iron Tongue clambered up onto a stone pillar and shouted at the top of his lungs, "Die, fools! You will turn and run and die before Iron Tongue's might!"

Lan felt the full unleashed power of that voice. The Voice. Even partially guarded magically against it, he felt the gut-level urge to obey the command. He prevented Inyx from turning and throwing herself on her sword.

"He is careless. He becomes . . . crazy." Rugga barely spoke. Noratumi moved closer and whispered to her. The woman quickly nodded. They moved to one side.

The tiny dramas being played out on the battlements of Wurnna didn't interest Lan. The wavering of the invisibility spells to either flank did. He concentrated on the western side, his magical powers insinuating themselves, turning, twisting, subverting. The party scaling the cliff flickered into sight.

"Iron Tongue," called one of his observers. "The western face."

"They receive a rocket. Now!"

The missile exploded yards from its target. Through squinted eyes, Lan saw flesh boil off still living skeletons. Dozens perished under the attack.

"The other face," he said quietly. "Don't forget the other cliff to the east."

Iron Tongue swiveled another of the rockets and launched it. This one went wild, going far off target. But Lan saw the true power of the projectiles. The exploding power stone disrupted the invisibility spell—he knew then that it distorted all magics within a certain radius. Even as he drew power to aid his own spells, so could the stone rob power when suddenly released.

The next rocket blew apart the hardy band clinging to the rock face.

"Do your worst, Claybore. You'll never take *my* city!"

Lan said softly to Inyx, "There is barely enough power stone left for five rockets. That won't be enough. Already new parties attack the heights."

"So? The spiders?"

"I'm afraid so. Especially now." He looked to the east. The commander of the new group moved with jerky movements that were only too familiar. This group would attain the heights over Wurnna. Kiska k'Adesina would see to it.

"Magic. Claybore attacks with magic!"

The cry pulled Lan Martak from a deep, dreamless sleep. He rolled over, freeing himself from both cloak and Inyx's embrace. He sat up and stared into the starless sky.

Starless?

"What is that demon of a sorcerer doing? He's blotted out the stars." Lan concentrated and sent his mote of light blazing into the firmament, only to have its brilliance snuffed out. The curtain of inky darkness slowly descended, threatening to cover the city.

"What's he doing?" Inyx stirred herself to full combat readiness, even though she knew this wasn't to be a battle of swords but of magics.

"I don't know. But let's see if he can contain this."

Lan drew on the power from the magical rock, formed it, shaped it into a lance, held the spear, and thrust it directly upward, twisting it and applying more and more pressure. When he thought his brain would explode with effort, the magical spear ripped through.

The sky ignited with the light of a million stars, once more normal.

"He uses the same magics I used to form the ebon dragons. I never realized they were so potent." Lan's words died when tornadoes of fire whipped across the plain in front of the main gates of Wurnna. Dancing and bobbing, those cyclones touched earth and life perished. Again he drew on the power stone and again he dissipated Claybore's magics.

"Can you keep this up for long?" Rugga and Noratumi had joined him on the battlement. Rugga's anxious question went unanswered as he concentrated on Claybore's next thrust in this magical duel.

Rain fell. Cold rain. Cold, burning rain. Every droplet seared and singed naked flesh, ate through stone, bored straight for the core of the planet. Lan slipped and stumbled, Inyx supporting him. He sapped her power, then Noratumi's, and finally Rugga's. He drew on all their inner strength to form an umbrella above the city. The rain mercifully stopped instants before the young mage knew he could no longer shield even himself from it.

"So," said Iron Tongue, boldly walking onto the battlement, "he tries again. This time I will fix him." Iron Tongue bellowed and chanted, cursed and conjured spells and sent the full force of his tongue-powered imprecations rumbling down the valley. Lan wondered if it affected Claybore at all, but if it stopped his grey-clad troops, the effort wasn't in vain.

"There will be more," Lan told Iron Tongue. "I can't stop it all. Even with Rugga's help, I can't. I doubt the full power of those remaining can hold Claybore off indefinitely."

"You may prove too weak. I will not. I am Iron Tongue, ruler of Wurnna." He threw his head back and laughed, the rolling guffaws mocking the very sky.

And as if offended, the sky retaliated.

Huge boulders fell from above, dropping onto buildings, smashing people and roads and anything else in their way.

"What's he doing now? Stop them, Lan. Nullify Claybore's spells."

"I can't, Inyx. Those are real. Claybore, or one of his pet mages, propels the rock magically, but the rocks are real. Too real."

Tiredness assailed him. He felt his knees shaking in reaction to the enormous powers that he had tapped, that he had allowed to flow through him. Lan knew k'Adesina had finally scaled the cliffs and established the sharpened edges of the pincer closing on Wurnna. Unless those heights were retaken, all would die within the city.

"The rockets, man, use the rockets." Rugga tugged at Iron Tongue's arm.

"There aren't any more. The last of the projectiles was used this afternoon." Iron Tongue appeared confused. "We . . . we can use the power stone from the streets. Rip it from the building foundations. Let the spires fall. We have enough."

Lan shook his head. What Iron Tongue advocated would take months of hard work. The power stone had become an integral part of the city, strong enough for building purposes but too diffuse magically for real defensive work.

"Another! Duck!"

A boulder twice the size of the first crashed into the center of the city. Shock waves raced outward. Even if the destruction to life and property hadn't been so severe, the falling rock would have taken its toll. Few inside the walls would fight if they were demoralized and fearful. Soon enough the mere thought of the empty sky would work its horror on them—every instant would be spent in dread of still another missile from heaven.

"We can't last a day like this," moaned Jacy Noratumi. He took Rugga's hand and pulled her close.

"You must," said Lan. "You must!" Even as he spoke he knew the city's life was numbered only in hours unless something was done to thwart the dismembered mage. The attack came from too many directions, both physical and magical. He needed to blunt one of those prongs before success could be achieved. He silently motioned to Inyx and Krek and they slipped away. Only one course of action suggested itself. It might be a fool's mission, but they had to try.

CHAPTER FIFTEEN

Rocks exploded like newborn suns throughout Wurnna. Even when Iron Tongue and his few remaining mages began the chants, made the spells, exerted all the power possible, the rain of stony death continued. Eventually the barrage stopped, not because of their action, but for lack of projectiles high atop the mountains.

"We have conquered them!" shrieked Iron Tongue, one fist waving at the sky. The other sorcerers backed away from their leader, shaking their heads. They knew the truth. They had failed; only fate had intervened in their behalf. Most of Wurnna lay in ruin. Left in command, Iron Tongue would soon allow all of it to be smashed into oblivion.

None questioned his right to rule. None dared oppose his wishes. None wanted the full force of his persuasive powers turned against him. Through the years they had seen strong men throw themselves on their swords at Iron Tongue's command. Women had ripped the throats from their infants because he had ordered it done. The voice—the Voice—was too strong. Even if he were insane, he ruled Wurnna.

Lan Martak saw and accepted this, but he drew aside Inyx and a few of the others for a quiet conference.

''When Claybore's troops get enough rock assembled again, the barrage will annihilate us. How long do you think it'll take to get the rocks assembled? Noratumi? Rugga?''

Jacy Noratumi glanced up at the heights and shuddered.

''This place,'' he said, ''should never have been built here. Why mages thought it could be defended is beyond me.''

''We defended it well until Claybore came along,'' said Rugga, an edge to her voice. ''We were many and strong. None scaled the heights without feeling the full force of our magics. And if we weakened, Iron Tongue urged climbers to simply step off to their death.''

Noratumi shook his head. All read his expression: A poor way to defend a city.

''You've not done so well protecting your own city-state,'' added Rugga.

''Bickering won't help,'' said Inyx. ''We need action. Lan thinks the spiders might aid us.''

''Never,'' scoffed Noratumi. ''We need action, all right. We need to put a sword through the heart of every grey-clad bastard on those mountain slopes.''

''He's right. The spiders will never leave their valley, even if they held any good feeling for us. Which they don't.'' Rugga's voice almost broke with emotion. She stared over the stony crenelation along the walkway and down the valley where all prior attacks had been mounted. Now only smouldering pits formed by the power stone rockets scarred the land. Claybore's troops had withdrawn beyond the effective range of Iron Tongue's Voice and let their numbers on the mountains do their work.

''Might I make a suggestion?'' piped up Krek. ''While I am most doubtful of assistance from Murrk, it can do no harm to inquire of him. Also, friend Jacy Noratumi is accurate in his appraisal of the situation. Continued rock-throwing will destroy the city long before any rescue might be made by my fellow arachnids.''

"So?"

"I propose we follow both schemes. One group scales the peaks, an easy task it seems to me, and removes the elevated danger. Force Claybore to send reinforcements. In that time, Lan might have persuaded Murrk to send aid."

Lan Martak thought it over. He ran fingers through his matted, dirty brown hair and absently wiped the grease and grime he encountered on his tunic. His mind sailed ahead, considering the options.

"Krek's right. Claybore is using a minimal amount of effort to destroy Wurnna. We've got to make him work harder if he wants to take us out."

"He cannot have many mages," said Rugga. "And he cannot do all this by himself."

"That's an avenue, also. Those remaining in Wurnna might attack at the periphery of Claybore's power, finding his assistants and badgering them. Drive them from their tasks, make them waver and be uncertain. Inyx, you and Jacy try the cliffs. Stop k'Adesina and her soldiers. Krek and I'll try to make it to the valley and back with some help."

Lan swallowed hard after he said this. Sending Inyx out with Jacy tore him in different directions. Emotionally he disliked the idea of their being together, fighting together, depending on one another, but he knew they forged the strongest team for the assault. His dealings with Krek and the spiders made him the most likely candidate for presenting the humans' case. Krek was his friend, but he didn't trust the arachnid to make the strongest case possible for the humans; Krek's thought processes often took bizarre turnings.

"Let Krek go alone. Stay in the city and aid us, Lan." Rugga fingers tightened on his sleeve. He saw the game she played. If he wanted to send Inyx out with Noratumi, then they could remain together.

"We do it as I outlined." He saw momentary tears

well in Inyx's eyes, then they vanished as she stiffened
to her task. In less than a minute she and Noratumi had
left to find a small band of trustworthy fighters able to
climb and fight.

"Krek? Let's go."

"Take me with you, then, Lan." Rugga's grip tightened on his arm until the fingers dug into his flesh. He
placed his hand gently atop hers.

"Wurnna needs defending. Your place is here. If we
can save this city, we will."

"And if you can't?"

"I'll be back for you." He was taken aback by the
intensity of her kiss. His lips tingled and his head spun
as he pulled away and left Rugga on the battlement.

At the postern gate, Krek finally spoke.

"You humans *do* have the strangest mating rituals."

Lan said nothing. At that instant he would have
gladly traded Krek and a million spiders for the chance
to accompany Inyx and fight beside her once again. The
gate slammed behind them with grim finality. He turned
and once again traversed the tunnel through the mountains.

"This narrow draw," Inyx said slowly. "It looks
suspiciously dangerous to me."

Noratumi stopped and motioned for the twenty warriors with them to halt. Silently he studied the vee-cut
in the rock. Inyx lightly touched his arm and pointed.
Tiny growths dotted the top of the rock with their spiny
stalks.

"It grows naturally in the mountains," he said. "I
see nothing."

"I don't see anything. I *feel* it."

"You're no mage."

"I don't have to be a mage, dammit!" she flared.
"Being in enough fights makes you sensitive to situations that are wrong. I smell a trap ahead."

"It's a good place," he agreed, "but I think you're

wrong. We're wasting time. Any trouble we encounter will be at their base camp at the foot of the cliffs."

Inyx held back as Noratumi signaled for an advance. She took aside one of the archers and whispered in his ear. His face contorted in a mixture of fear and confusion, but he did as she ordered. He nocked an arrow and waited.

The trap was sprung almost immediately when the lead scout entered the notch in the rocks. The spiny plants she had noticed erupted out and downward. The scout had lightning-swift reflexes. His sword flashed out and speared the plant on his left. The one falling from the right skewered his arm. His agonized shriek pierced the cold silence of the mountain range.

The man turned and thrashed about, vainly struggling to pull free the plant. He was dead before his fingers even closed about the stalk.

"Poison," said Inyx, not in the least happy that she'd been vindicated. The archer pulled and released in a smooth motion. His arrow caught another clump of poisoned spine weed in midair, knocking it from its path toward Noratumi's head.

Jacy Noratumi backpedaled quickly, avoiding another flight of the deadly plants.

"Now what?" asked a woman nearby. "I'm not going through there. Not as long as I might end up like poor Langmur." The scout still twitched on the floor of the notch, long dead in the brain but the body still not convinced.

"There's no way through, except for this. We'll have to turn back and take the other fork."

"That's going to cost us hours, Jacy," protested Inyx. "Wurnna doesn't have the time." Even as she spoke a new barrage of boulders was magically arced up and over onto the city.

"Maybe Rugga and the others can . . ." But Noratumi knew that was a faint hope. The first of the falling rocks deflected away from its target. The next came closer. The third still closer. Even as they argued, the mages remaining inside the city walls weakened from repeated use of their power.

Inyx decided quickly.

"Fire-arrows. Ignite them and launch them through the gap. Whoever rigged this trap—and I suspect Silvain's gentle touch—can't have planned for a full assault."

"Why fire-arrows?"

"Heat. There's no way a trip plate could be placed in the rocky floor. Do you see any wires?" Seeing Noratumi's answer, she added, "A small magical spell to sense body heat, a few spring-loaded devices on the boulders, and that's all."

"I hope you're right."

After the seventh fire-arrow blazed through the gap, the poisoned spines stopped falling from their hiding spots. But still Inyx wasn't satisfied. She made the archers shoot another fifty arrows before being convinced this wasn't a more subtle trap. And even then, she insisted on being the first through. If she'd underestimated Silvain, let it be her life that was forfeit.

Safely on the other side of the cut, she motioned for the rest to follow.

At a quick trot, the small band followed the tracks left by the grey-clads on their way upward. Within sight of both the camp at the base of the cliff and the winding path upward, Inyx heard boot leather grinding on rock.

Alberto Silvain stood in the path, just out of bow range, hands resting on slim hips, his legs widespread. While she couldn't clearly see his face, she sensed the smirk.

"Inyx, we meet again," he called. "I rather thought you'd have stopped to admire the flora of this backwater planet. You continually surprise me."

"I'll do more than that. I'll kill you, you murdering bastard!"

"Inyx," warned Noratumi, restraining her.

"Yes, your barbarian friend is right. Another step and you won't take a second." From all around rose grey-clad archers.

Even as they drew back their bows, Noratumi gave the signal to his own to fire. Arrows flashed back and forth in the air. Some struck their enemies' shafts and deflected them. Still others fell harmlessly. A few found their marks, either by magic or skill.

"You realize your dilemma, Inyx," came Silvain's mocking voice. "I guard the way up. You must stop dear Kiska and her captive mage from dropping her rocks and I prevent it. If you tarry, Wurnna will be reduced to rubble. Please. Surrender. I shall treat you honorably." The laugh that accompanied the words put all doubt out of her mind as to what Silvain meant.

"What now?" asked Noratumi.

Inyx had to admit she didn't know.

Lan Martak tapped the energy from the power stone more and more. The bracelet circling his wrist and the necklace bobbing with his every step turned warm to the touch, but his muscles worked smoothly and he felt no fatigue. He and Krek made it back to the valley of the spiders in less time than ever before. The terrain between the massif guarding Wurnna and the valley had become too well known to him due to the number of times he'd traversed it of late.

"Why do you return? For more of the rock?" The spider dangling above Lan's head clashed mandibles together in a ferocious display. Lan no longer feared such demonstrations. He had magical powers that far surpassed mere physical ones now.

"We need aid," he said in a straightforward manner. There was too little time to dance around the issue.

"Friend Lan Martak, this is not the way," Krek told him. The spider bounded aloft, deftly catching one of

the web strands and scampering along it to hang beside
the Webmaster. The two chittered and screeched in
high-pitched spider talk while Lan impatiently waited.
Nervous, he paced. Upset, he smashed rocks with tiny
spells. And the hours passed.

"Krek," he called out, "what's happening?"

"Murrk is unconvinced. I do not blame him, either.
There is scant loyalty to be drawn upon in this matter.
It certainly does not bring honor to the web defending
humans from their own kind." Krek paused, then asked,
"Would you allow Murrk to eat any humans he catches?"

When Lan didn't answer, Krek said sadly, "I thought
as much. The negotiations go slowly. We might take a
short while yet."

Lan shook his head. Krek's idea of a "short while"
might be a week or more. To the arachnid, he had just
begun the discussion with the Webmaster and over nine
hours had passed. The sun dipped below the high mountain peaks and cast deep shadows across the valley.

With night came increasing uneasiness. Lan no longer
saw the spiders in the web but only heard their clacks
and whistles and chitters. What bothered him most
was the growing sensation of something amiss. He
finally decided it had nothing to do with the spiders; as
long as Krek accompanied him there was little danger
to him.

He smiled ruefully. Rugga had been right. His presence wasn't really needed here. Murrk wouldn't even
speak to him. Still, Lan thought he might be of assistance if Krek faltered in the talks.

"But there's something more," he said aloud to
himself. The sensation hanging in the air was similar to
the humid heaviness before a summer thunderstorm.
Lan reached inside and pulled forth his mote of light,
sending the faithful scout forth to investigate. In only
seconds the dancing pinpoint of light returned for him
to read the warning of impending danger.

"Krek!" he bellowed. "Warn the spiders. Claybore's getting ready to destroy a retaining dam high in the mountains. This entire valley will be flooded!"

"Water? You say water?" Responding wasn't Krek but Murrk. "The humans do this terrible deed?"

"Claybore does it. That's why we oppose him," said Lan. "You've got to reach high ground." The mote whirled about his head in a quick orbit and he read the rest of Claybore's plan. "But be careful to stay out of your webs. He is going to fire them."

"Water? Then fire! Nooooo!" The echo reached the full length of the valley.

A dull plop marked Krek dropping from the web to stand beside him. The brown-haired youth stared off into the distance, not seeing with his eyes as much as with his mind.

"You are not inventing this danger to frighten Murrk into helping, are you?" Krek slumped down. "Oh woe! Fire. Water. Why do you humans so enjoy such nasty things?"

"Claybore's not what you'd call human," Lan said distractedly. "I think I might be able to stop him. With a little help, that is."

"Oh?"

"The dam can be protected. The fires require a considerable bit more magic on my part, but maybe, just maybe something can be done."

"Do it, friend Lan Martak. I have come to like these brothers of mine. Murrk, especially. For a Webmaster he is considerate and capable, even if he does strike me as obdurate at times. Actually, when you take into account all he has to do . . ."

"Never mind that, Krek. Get them aloft into the webs in case I can't stop the dam from being torn apart."

"But the fires."

"First things first. Claybore plans to drive them into

the webs and then burn them out of the air. If the dam holds, he might reconsider the fires.''

"A faint hope. We are all doomed. Doomed, I say.'' Krek began sniffling, tears forming at the corners of his dun-colored eyes. Lan ignored the mood shift. He had work to do. Hard work.

He didn't even remember sinking to the ground to sit tailor-fashion. The first effort to block Claybore's magic failed. Lan tried to spread the mote of light into a curtain once more, but this time the energies were too thin to hold the enormous weight of a dam. All Claybore needed was a magical spear thrust through the dam under water level; a thousand motes plugging the hole wouldn't stay the tons of water rushing outward.

Lan changed his mode of attack.

And in front of him floated the ghostly visage he had come to know and hate.

"So, my petty apprentice mage, you think to stop me in this little task?''

"I will, Claybore.'' Lan's gaze didn't waver as he stared directly into those hollow eye sockets. The tiny whirlwinds of red no longer inspired fear. He had matured and Claybore no longer menaced him—in that fashion. Nor did the other sorcerer attempt to use the ruby death shafts. The duel became more subtle, but nonetheless deadly.

Claybore's attention wavered for a moment. Lan instinctively knew that tremendous spells were being conjured. His friend the mote of light reported back: water elemental.

The undine stirred in the muck at the bottom of the lake formed by the dam, stretched her muscles, shivered, and rippled with reborn power. The water about her boiled and blackened and she expanded, grew in stature, in power, finally *lived* after so many centuries of discontented slumber in the lake bottom.

The command impressed on her dull brain held her

captive, but the command was a simple one. Swim. A water elemental did that best above all else. She swam. Directly for the base of the dam built in ancient days by those of Wurnna. The cold stone wouldn't deter her. She was powerful, aided by powerful magics.

All this the mote reported to Lan Martak. For the briefest of instants, he quailed at the thought of what he must do. Fear welled up within him, then subsided as reason took control of his emotions. He did what had to be done.

His chants filled the valley of spiders with a plaintive, eerie sound. His hands moved constantly, weaving the complex binding spells in the air before him. And above all, his mind wrestled with the summoning, power coming from the gem-bracelet and necklace—and from deep within his own soul.

The salamander screamed vengeance as it formed in the air above the valley. Vaguely aware of the consternation among the spiders, Lan could do nothing to ease their fears. Conjuring elementals required total concentration; they were cunning creatures not easily bound and all too willing to turn on the mage summoning them.

"Into the lake," Lan ordered his fire elemental. The salamander hissed in rage and railed against the command that would cause its brief existence to be snuffed out. Lan's control lacked much of that shown by Claybore, but the control was adequate. Reluctantly, the fire elemental arched in the air, a sinuosity of flame and blinding light that turned night into day, then launched itself directly for the retaining dam and the undine behind it.

Fire and water do not mix. As the elementals collided, water with fire, huge columns of steam rose to support the nighttime sky. The female undine fought recklessly with male salamander, but the outcome was never in question. Both snuffed out of existence.

Lan fell supine on the valley floor, panting, his face flushed. He blinked sweat from his eyes and peered up at Krek. With voice cracking, he asked, "Did I stop him?"

"There is no water in the valley."

"I stopped him. I stopped Claybore!" Lan exulted for a moment, then realized that the battle was not won by a single round. Claybore did these conjurings only to slow him. Every second spent fighting elementals and worrying over new and more diabolical traps allowed Kiska k'Adesina time to drop more boulders on feckless Wurnna.

Weakened as he was, Lan Martak took the time to do a quick survey of the valley. The dam had been weakened by the swift but brutal struggle of elementals; the important point was that it held. Cracks formed along important junctures but the dam held.

"Any signs of fire in the web?" he asked.

"Only a few from the fire elemental raging above. Those portions of the web have been isolated and new supports are being spun." Lan again sent out his magical scout. The arachnids coated endangered portions of their web with a sticky chemical similar to that used on their hunting webs. This retarded the fire long enough to give them time to spin new supporting cables and then cut loose the burning sections.

"No lives were lost."

"But time has been stolen away," said Krek. "Claybore manipulates us all like pieces on a game board. He occupies our time with fear—of fire and water, oh, the horror of it all!—and cares not if we perish. If so, he is content. If not, he has gained the time to further his schemes elsewhere. He must be stopped, friend Lan Martak."

"I'm trying. And you've got to try again with Murrk. Without the aid of the spiders, I don't think Wurnna can survive."

"The dam will break soon," came the Webmaster's shrill voice. Lan spun around to see the giant spider hanging from a strand a few feet above his head.

"You have time to fix it now."

"We cannot fix such things. In ancient times that structure was built by the humans to gain access to this valley and the rock mines they value so. We lack the skill to repair it."

Lan began to see another quirk of history on this world. The mages of Wurnna had built the dam to reach the power stone mines, but the spiders had moved in once the yearly floods were stemmed.

"You can leave the valley," he said, knowing what response he was likely to get. He wasn't disappointed.

"Never! This is our home! For centuries this is our web!"

"With Wurnna gone, defeated by Claybore, I suppose there'll be no one left to repair the dam."

Murrk considered the ramifications for a short while—a virtual snap decision on the part of the spider—and then said, "If we fight off the interloper soldier humans, will the other humans repair the cracks and insure our safety?"

"They'd be so grateful for the help, I'm sure they would do it willingly."

Murrk whistled and clicked and bobbed about for ten minutes. In that time the already dark sky darkened even more with the bulk of hundreds of spiders.

Lan Martak had his relief force. If only they weren't too late to save Wurnna.

CHAPTER SIXTEEN

"There's no chance for attack," said Jacy Noratumi. "Look. They pick us off one by one. We must retreat."

"That's cut off, too," Inyx pointed out. The tip of her sword indicated the various strategic positions occupied by Silvain's archers. As long as the greys held the high ground, Inyx and her company could neither attack nor retreat.

Even as she spoke, one of Silvain's men tried to go up the narrow path leading to the top of the mountain. One of her own archers rose and let fly a deadly shaft. The arrow flew straight and true; the man on the path died—and so did Inyx's archer. A dozen hidden positions loosed arrows directly into the chest and belly.

"They can afford to trade one for one since they outnumber us," Noratumi said glumly. "And there is scant we can do."

Inyx hated having to agree. They'd be cut down if they attempted to return to Wurnna. A frontal assault was equally as suicidal. And staying only allowed Kiska k'Adesina time to move boulders atop the mountain for Claybore and his mages to scoot over the city and drop, letting gravity do most of the work.

"Keep firing and play it safe," was all she could

suggest. The woman studied the situation and, for the greater part of a day, observed no weakness. Near twilight the next day, however, she pointed out certain flaws in the armed array facing them.

"Attack is still out of the question," said Noratumi, "but escape appears more likely. Does Silvain toy with us?"

"I don't think Silvain is even in camp," she said. "I believe he took another route around the cliff and has rejoined Claybore."

"If that is so, perhaps k'Adesina has also left her post up there." Jacy pointed above to where tiny antlike creatures—workers—toiled to line up heavy boulder after boulder along the rim.

"That can only mean the main attack is imminent." She considered their alternatives and all looked equally bleak. "We go back to Wurnna. Now."

Noratumi silently signaled those near to pass along the order. Smashing repeatedly against the force guarding the path up the mountainside accomplished nothing. Inyx took every step away imagining what an arrow driving into her spine might feel like. While there were short, quick engagements, most of her force succeeded in regaining the trail leading back to Wurnna.

"What if this is another trap?" asked one of the archers.

"We have to take the chance that Silvain is no longer commanding that detachment," said Noratumi. "It's a better chance than we had."

"But the possibility of traps. . . ."

"Exists," admitted Inyx. "We also know to stay over long means our death." She hit the rocky trail at an easy lope and quickly outdistanced the others. Being alone helped her think of the things that were important; she ignored the possibility of a cleverly laid trap.

Lan. He must have known her mission was a long shot with a one-in-a-million chance of succeeding. Was his trip to the valley of spiders any less of a clutching at feeble hope? She doubted it. By dawn Wurnna would again find the rocks descending from on high. In less than a day Claybore would have smashed the city to dust.

What then? Inyx didn't want to think about it. Claybore's conquest of still another world would be total.

The diminished band reached Wurnna a half-hour before the pale pinks of dawn lit the horizon. Inyx felt no joy at the sight of a new day, for this one would be filled with death and destruction unlike any she'd witnessed before along the Cenotaph Road.

"Why don't they use their damned rocks?" Jacy Noratumi paced along the walkway, hands clasped behind his back. Now and then he reared back to study the mountains on either side of the fortress. In plain sight were twin rows of boulders large enough to smash the city to gravel, but Claybore refrained from launching them.

"Perhaps he is occupied elsewhere," suggested Rugga, hovering near Noratumi.

"Or he might be tired. He must tire like other mages. He has so few other sorcerers to aid him that he might require time to rest."

Inyx scoffed at this, saying, "He is immortal. Even Terrill wasn't able to kill him. His power is limited, true, but there has never been a time when he's held off attacking through weakness. He plays a war of nerves with us. He lets us see the boulders long enough to anticipate. He breaks our will to defend Wurnna."

"It's working," was all Noratumi said.

Iron Tongue came striding up, looking as if he had won the war and ruled all the world. Inyx discounted the man totally now; he had lost contact with reality. While his words still carried their magical power, thanks to the tongue resting in his mouth, those words were confused and of little effect now.

"He runs from us. I have won!" the demented mage crowed. He opened his mouth and thrust out his metallic tongue in the direction of Claybore's encampment at the far end of the canyon. It caught the noonday sun's rays and transmuted them into dark and sinister light, as that reflected from a polished coffin. Inyx had to look away.

"Look. In the plain." Rugga rushed forward, pointing.

"A trick. Kill the bastard!" roared Noratumi. The archers sprang to their feet and loosed volley after volley of arrows. They turned aside harmlessly before touching either Claybore's skull or torso or the mechanical carrying them.

"Hold!" boomed the dismembered sorcerer's voice. "I would parlay."

"See? He surrenders to me. To me, Iron Tongue of Wurnna!" The cackling drowned out Claybore's next words.

" . . . above you, unused. But at any time they can be brought down. My terms are just and fair. I want my tongue. In exchange I shall grant all within Wurnna their freedom."

"What of the city?" called Rugga.

"It must be destroyed, but all within shall remain alive."

Inyx shook her head vehemently. Noratumi and Rugga were slower to admit that Claybore plotted a trap.

"Why offer us a truce at all?" asked Inyx. "He can crush us with his boulders. He has the power. Claybore is not one to refrain from wanton violence."

"He wants the tongue intact. Using the aerial bombardment might harm it," said Rugga. "That is the only reason I can think of. I say, give it to him. We can fight him another day."

"He won't keep his word," blazed Inyx. "He will

kill us the instant he has the tongue. Its use will make him infinitely stronger. You can imagine how potent will be the spells cast using it. Look at what *he* does with it." The distaste in her voice brought Iron Tongue's head swiveling around.

"You speak of me, wench? I am considering Claybore's offer. There is a certain justice in what he offers."

"Dammit, you just said you'd won. Will you surrender so quickly?" Inyx saw that arguing with a madman accomplished nothing. Iron Tongue's mood and thought flipped from minute to minute.

"He will beg me for the tongue. Yes, I like that idea. Wurnna will survive, if he begs me for my tongue." He thrust out the parody of a tongue in Claybore's direction once more, somehow managing to cause a grotesquely unnatural ripple to flow from one metallic end to the other. Tiny blue sparks lapped at the edges before it vanished back into the mage's mouth.

Inyx leaned forward, hands on the protective stone of the battlement, too angry to speak. It wasn't her place to decide for those of Wurnna. Iron Tongue was still their leader, demented or not. Rugga might seize power. She turned and looked at the woman, weighing the chance this might happen. A quick assassinating stab with a dagger into Iron Tongue's kidney would leave the rulership vacant. But Rugga obviously had other goals now. She and Jacy Noratumi stood too close, eyed each other in a way Inyx understood all too well. Rugga wanted nothing more to do with Wurnna and leadership. She wanted only Noratumi.

"Fight," Inyx said, her voice almost too low to be heard. "Fight to the death. It's cleaner than what he offers. He will never allow us to walk away."

Iron Tongue rocked forward, bent slightly at the hips, as if summoning up the energy to give in to Claybore. Inyx's hand rested on her sword hilt. She wondered if a quick draw and a powerful slash across the throat would decapitate Iron Tongue. She doubted it. There would have to be a second cut, but the first might silence him enough to prevent use of the full force of his tongue.

An instant before she unsheathed and executed, hideous screams came cascading down from above. Startled, the dark-haired woman looked up. Then she let out a loud whoop of joy.

"Lan did it! The spiders!"

The soldiers either leaped or were tossed off the mountains by the score. Where once there had been boulders falling, now the air filled with flailing, screaming bodies. Darker forms dotted the cliffs, moving upward with agile grace.

"A boulder!" came the warning. "The boulders fly!"

One did smash into Wurnna, but the rest simply rolled off the canyon rim to plunge impotently to the floor some distance from the city. Inyx spun and looked out at the plain stretching in front of the city gates. Claybore balanced atop his mechanical as if stunned by the sudden turn of events. When he rattled off, shouting orders as he went, his troops milled in obvious disarray.

"Iron Tongue," said Inyx. "Use the Voice. Stop the troops from running away."

"Halt!" The word rolled like thunder down the canyon. The grey-clads froze in their tracks. In spite of two figures going through the ranks, flogging and kicking, the majority of the soldiers stood frozen in their tracks.

"Those two," muttered Noratumi. "Silvain and k'Adesina?"

"Probably. Claybore called them in for what was to be his moment of triumph."

"Why'd you want the troops to stand? Now they can wheel and fight. We're in no shape to fend off another assault." Rugga wore every piece of the power stone jewelry she had and still it seemed to give her little enough energy to conjure. The toll on her strength had been extreme while keeping Claybore's magics at bay.

"Wait. Just wait." Inyx knew how Krek thought. If the giant arachnid commanded those on the heights, as she suspected he did, there would soon be a new element introduced into battle at the floor of the canyon. When spiders came crashing down on thick strands of webstuff, she knew the heights were secure. The spiders gathered, at first by ones and twos, then by dozens, to move away from Wurnna and into the frozen ranks of Claybore's army.

Even the power of Iron Tongue's command faded as raw terror shook the men and women facing eight-foot spiders with clacking mandibles and a ferocity little known outside the insect kingdom.

The carnage was great and the confusion in Claybore's ranks even greater. Inyx found herself delighting in the sight of blood flowing in trickles, streams, rivers. To her left Iron Tongue stood stunned and uncomprehending. To her right Jacy and Rugga clung to one another. Inyx might gain vicarious revenge and savor the destruction, but none of the other humans did.

"They deserve this," Inyx tried to explain. "They tried to destroy your city. They did destroy Bron."

"But this . . ." croaked Rugga, turning away.

"This ends the physical threat," came a new voice. "But Claybore will not give up this easily."

"Lan!" Inyx rushed to him and gave him the hero's kiss he deserved. He pushed her away, oddly distant.

"The battle is just beginning. Rugga, assemble all the mages. Claybore will fight like a cornered rat now. We must be ready. We must keep the tongue away from him at all costs."

To be out of sight of the bloodshed wreaked by the spiders, Rugga was happy to go on any mission, no matter how trivial. Only Lan Martak realized that the ferocity of battle had yet to reach a climax.

• • •

"Look at the death they caused. The grey-clads will never return. Not ever." Iron Tongue stood and gloated. The others uneasily stared out at the canyon stretching away from the city. While Claybore's physical army may have been destroyed by the spiders, who now had returned to their valley, his magical senses were untouched. What worried Lan and the others the most was the lack of aggression shown by the dismembered mage.

"He plots something more diabolical than ever before," said Rugga. "I feel the air thickening about us."

Lan sensed this also, but discounted it as nervous foreboding. Whatever magics Claybore unleashed on them wouldn't carry advanced warning.

"Are you all right?" asked Inyx, putting her hands on his shoulders and pressing her body to his back. She rested her cheek on his broad shoulder. "Ever since you came back from the valley of spiders you've been distant."

"I conjured an elemental," he said, knowing it meant little to her. "That's one of the most potent of all sorceries and I did it, hardly without thinking. I dipped down and drew power from within—and from the power stone—and countered Claybore's water elemental with a fire elemental."

"Heavy magic," she said, obviously unaware of the tinkering with nature such a conjuration required.

"I did it so easily. Such power—and I don't want it!" He held his hands before him and simply stared at them. These weren't the hands he remembered. The work-thickenings were gone. These hands had turned soft and seemed incapable of properly wielding a sword, yet Lan Martak saw more on, within, around his fingers and palms. A radiance welled up from inside, pale and golden and more potent than even the strongest of sinews. He had lost a minor physical talent while gaining a major magical and psychic one.

"The Fates have chosen you to carry the fight to Claybore, to stop him," Inyx said softly. "Destiny, luck, call it what you will. You are the only one capable of doing it."

"But I'm not a mage," he protested.

"You weren't," she corrected. "You are now. Your talents were hidden, but the many transitions between worlds have brought forth your true power."

"Am I still human?" he asked in a voice barely loud enough to hear. "Is any sorcerer human?"

Inyx answered by gently turning him around and kissing him.

"You're human," she pronounced. "And I love you."

He returned the kiss and held her, feeling the world could stop now and he'd be happy for all eternity. But the mood shattered when he sensed a stirring of magic.

"Claybore!" he cried. Rugga and the few remaining mages were already on their feet, staring out into the emptiness, wondering what devilment Claybore produced.

They didn't wait long to find out.

A warrior dressed in flame strode out. No human this, he towered a hundred feet above the walls of Wurnna. Mighty hands clutched a sword that no score of men might lift. Muscles rippling and sending out dancing tongues of fire, the giant swung the sword.

Lan and the others tried to ward off the blow. The sword grated and screeched and cut through stone, sending vast clouds of dust into the air. Wherever the sword touched stone, it turned molten and burned with insane intensity. None of Wurnna approached closer than a bowshot; none could endure the searing flame.

The giant bellowed out his hatred for all within the city and took a mighty overhead swing. The blade sundered the wall with a deafening crash.

"Lan," gasped Rugga, the sweat of fear popping out

on her forehead and gathering the dust, "how do we stop it? No weakness is to be found. Our spells have no effect."

The young mage studied, probed, lightly tested Claybore's monster for some clue. In its way this was a simpler magical construct than an elemental; it was also more difficult to counter. Lan knew an elemental would be a useless conjuration. Claybore wanted him to waste his efforts in ways producing little effect.

Lan clapped his hands and sent his dancing mote of light straight down into the ground at the giant's feet. The mote spun in ever-widening circles, boring, chewing up the very earth. Lan's mind probed downward into the ground, summoning darkness to counter the flame. The pit widened and the burning giant was forced to retreat out of sword range of the city.

"Lan," said Inyx, tugging at his sleeve. "The giant. There's something about him that's familiar."

"I know. It's Alberto Silvain."

Inyx recoiled in shock, thinking Lan's exertions had somehow caused his mind to snap. Then she looked more carefully at the giant's features. Bloated, vastly out of proportion, hidden by curtains of fire, but still she saw the resemblance.

"It *is* Silvain," she said, awe tingeing her voice. "But how does he do it?"

Lan ignored her now, concentrating on the pit. He worked it so that it stretched from one side of the canyon to the other, preventing the giant from crossing to again menace the city. But this was only a temporary measure; both he and Claybore knew it. The first round finished a draw.

"Prepare to launch a bolt of pure energy directly at the giant's chest," he ordered Rugga and the pathetic few huddling nearby. Sorcerers tended to be arrogant. The spirit of the Wurnna mages had been broken long ago. All he hoped for was some small additional backing. The brunt of this battle was his and his alone.

"Iron Tongue," whispered Inyx, "tell the giant to stand still. Don't let him move. You did it before. With the grey soldiers. Do it again." She was heartened to see the demented ruler puff up and look out onto the battlefield. His understanding of reality had fled, but some tasks still pleasured him.

"Die!" cried the mage. The word exploded from his mouth, backed by the full power of the tongue. Lan stumbled and had to support himself under the onslaught of that command. Iron Tongue might be insane, but the power of his tongue remained.

The effect on the giant convinced Lan that the battle might be winnable. He hadn't counted on the potent effects of the tongue Claybore so ardently sought to recover. The giant that was Alberto Silvain stumbled and lurched as if drunk on some heady wine. While still countering the force of Iron Tongue's command, the giant was vulnerable.

Lan Martak took full advantage to send the deadly bolt of energy the others had forged directly into Silvain's chest. The bolt appeared to be the largest lightning strike seen by humanity; to Lan it was a spear with a razor-sharp point driving straight for Silvain's heart. Not content with this, Lan diverted a bit of his power to further widen the vast cavity in the ground.

When the spear struck dead-center in his chest, Silvain let out a roar rivaling an erupting volcano. And, as in a volcano, torrents of hot lava exploded outward from him. This lava was the giant's lifeblood. Larger-than-life hands clutching vainly at the energy bolt piercing his flesh, Silvain sank to his knees.

"Martak," boomed the single name from his lips. It combined admiration, accusation, and condemnation all in that instant.

Lan widened the hole until the dirt began crumbling

under Silvain's knees. The giant fought to stay upright on his knees, to avoid falling into the limitless pit in front of him.

Iron Tongue let go another command to die that caused the flames leaping and cavorting along Silvain's limbs to extinguish like candles in a hurricane.

"Martak," Silvain repeated, then convulsively heaved the immense sword at Wurnna's battlements. Lan took the opportunity to enlarge the bottomless hole a few inches further. The flaming giant fell forward into it, twisting and struggling, then grew smaller and smaller, cooler and cooler, then vanished from sight.

Lan let out a gasp of relief that was replaced by stark terror when he blinked and saw the thrown sword inexorably moving toward him. The weapon moved as if dipped in honey, but it moved. Spells bounced off it. The dancing light mote couldn't touch it. Nothing deflected it.

"Out of the way," he commanded, knowing this might be Wurnna's doom. Claybore had counted on him attacking the wrong weapon. He had sacrificed Silvain in order to deliver this weapon. Silvain was a pawn now discarded; the sword carried magics Lan couldn't even guess at.

"I shall stop it," declared Iron Tongue. The ruler stood proudly on the battlement, chest bared as if daring Claybore to make the attempt. The sword moved smoothly, slowly, an unstoppable evil force.

Iron Tongue sucked in a lungful of air, then wove the command for the sword to vanish. It never wavered in its painstakingly slow journey toward Iron Tongue and Wurnna.

"Stop, I say. I command you. I am Iron Tongue. You can't ignore my command. Stop, *stop!*"

The huge sword point pierced Iron Tongue's chest. Like a branding iron through snow it came on, his flesh not even retarding the magical weapon's progress. Iron

Tongue twitched and weakly fought, a new command on his lips. Mouth falling open in death, the sorcerer's tongue obscenely dangled out.

"It's aimed for me," Lan said, pushing Inyx away. "Go join Jacy and the others. I don't want you close by."

"No, Lan, we're in this together."

He didn't argue. With a wave of his hand he conjured a shock wave that lifted her from her feet and tossed her off the battlements. She landed below in a pile of rubble. He couldn't even take the time to see if the fall had injured her. Even if it had, the fall was less likely to kill than the magical device he now faced.

The sword passed entirely through Iron Tongue, finally allowing the dead mage to slump to the stone walkway. As if guided by an unseen hand, the point turned and directed itself for Lan's midsection. Spell after spell he tried, all fruitlessly. His mind worked at top speed, trying to understand what Claybore had done. Then he had it. The spells fell into their proper place; his hands moved in the proper orbits; the chants sounded right.

The sword struck.

Lan screamed, his concentration gone as excruciating pain lashed his senses. He jerked away as it pinked just under his eye and felt the sword dig deeper into his flesh, his bone. He futilely grabbed at the sword blade with his hands, knowing even as he did so that no physical force would move the magical from its course. The sword point dug deeper into cheek, burrowing into the jawbone, driving for the back of his head where the point might sever the spinal column.

Lan couldn't stop the deadly advance; the joined forces of the remaining mages of Wurnna did. Rugga built on what Lan had started, forging a parrying force that turned the blade at the last possible instant.

"Destroy it!" shrieked Rugga. "Destroy Claybore's evil sword!"

Her anger and hatred flowered and added supplemental power to the spell she had guided. While weakened, the sorcerers of Wurnna found enough strength to shatter the blade. As it had sailed, so did it explode. Ruptured pieces turned slow cartwheels, barely moving, still deadly. Only when the last had embedded harmlessly in stone or deep in the earth did Rugga and Inyx rush forward to tend to Lan.

"Oh, no, by all the Fates, no," Inyx said over and over. She stood in shock at the sight. The lower right portion of Lan's jaw had been sheared away; his mouth was a bloody ruin. Thick spurts of his life juices blossomed and washed down his neck and chest.

"Claybore's revenge must be sweet," said Rugga, the bitterness there for all to hear. "He's cut out the tongue of his most powerful adversary. Lan Martak will never again utter a spell."

Inyx bent to staunch the bleeding. If Lan would never speak again, at least she could save his life. His eyelids fluttered up and glassy eyes softened at the sight of her, then he lapsed into unconsciousness.

CHAPTER SEVENTEEN

"Do something," pleaded Inyx. "He's dying." The
woman's crude and usually effective first aid hadn't
staunched the geysering flow of blood from Lan's jaw,
where arteries had been clipped by the sword. He no
longer made bubbling noises of pain. His body refused
to believe such agony was possible and rejected any
further misery.

But Inyx felt it fully for him. He'd been a handsome
man, young, vital, quick of wit and quicker with his
friendship and love. Now he lay with the lower right
half of his jaw cut away. His tongue had vanished along
with bone and teeth and palate, making only deep-
throated sounds possible now. Lan Martak had lapsed
into a state closer to coma than consciousness; he didn't
need to talk.

"He is dying," came the mocking words. "I can
save him. Give me the tongue and I will save your
lover." The image of Claybore's skull and torso floated
a few feet away. Inyx knew this was only illusion, that
the sorcerer remained safely hidden away where none
might physically reach him.

The offer tempted her sorely. Lan's life for the worthless tongue in a dead mage's mouth. Then she heard

soft rustlings of silk. She turned and saw Krek mounting the perpendicular stone wall as if it had stairs cut into it. The soft sounds came from the fur on his legs brushing as he walked.

"Friend Inyx," the spider said simply. He had taken in all that had occurred with one swift glance. "I feel as you do for our fallen friend, but what was his mission?"

"To stop Claybore," she said, her voice choked. Then, firmer with resolve, she glared at Claybore's fleshless skull and defiantly said, "Burn in all the Lower Places. You won't get the tongue!"

"He is dying. I can save him."

"He dies thwarting you. What more can any warrior ask? He died honorably, nobly, for a cause that means something."

"It means nothing!" blared the skull. "Nothing, do you hear!"

A wicked smile crossed Inyx's lips.

"You won't get the tongue. He stopped you. Darell-Lan-Martak stopped Silvain and now he's stopped you."

Claybore's response chilled her. She'd hoped for a moment of rage from the sorcerer. It didn't come. He laughed without humor.

"The tongue will be mine. You can't stop me now. Those few pitiful mages remaining cannot conjure a fraction as well as I do. Silvain died for me. Do you think there are others any less willing? Are you ready to face still another giant?"

"While it might be true that your conjuration powers exceed those shown by the Wurnna sorcerers," said Krek, "it is within their power to destroy the tongue before you can recover it. You shall lose its use, even if you do conquer this entire world. Of what use is such a Pyhrric victory?"

Again Claybore surprised them with his reaction.

He laughed louder, harder than ever before.

"The tongue is important, but I have won. Oh, yes, worms, I have won. He is dead." Ruby beams flashed from empty sockets to lightly brush across Lan's body. The man twitched but could not cry out in pain. "More important, my agents on other worlds have been active. While you tried your pitiful efforts against me on this world, they have been successful elsewhere. Soon enough, arms and legs will be mine."

"You won't have a tongue or a face!" taunted Inyx, but deep inside she felt sickness mounting. Their triumphs seemed pathetic in the face of Claybore's victories. Destroying the flesh from his skull and holding the tongue did not prevent him from becoming more powerful through the regaining of other bodily parts. Even if he lied, Lan's life slowly slipped away.

"I will come for the tongue." The image vanished.

For long minutes none moved, then Rugga motioned for the other mages to join her.

"He must be healed," she said, indicating Lan's limp form. "Bringing the dead back to life is beyond our power, in spite of what those of Bron have claimed for so long, but saving a life might not be."

The mages chanted, hummed, made magical signs in the air that burned with fiery intensity and left the odor of brimstone, but Lan got no better. While Inyx thought the slow consumption by death had been halted, they did him no favors preserving him at this level. He had been a vital man, a vibrant one full of life. To leave him like this was a travesty. Better she drive a dagger through his noble heart.

"Stay your hand, friend Inyx," said the spider. "There is one course of action you have not taken."

"What? What is it?" she demanded, eyes wide and imploring.

"I do not know if it will work, but it seems most logical. You see, there is a symmetry to the universe that we arachnids often ponder. Perhaps it comes from our love of geometrically symmetrical webs. We spin and weave and—"

"Krek!"

"Oh, yes. I shall try it and see." The spider lumbered over to Iron Tongue's body and used his front legs to roll the corpse onto its back. The dead mage's head lolled grotesquely to one side, the tongue so eagerly sought by Claybore thrusting from between bloated lips. Krek used his front talons to separate the lips and open the mouth. Bending down until the serrated tips of his mandibles were deep inside, he snipped.

The spider jumped back, a shrill screech piercing the air. The contact with the magical tongue had caused fat blue sparks to erupt forth, burning both dead lips and living spider. But Krek held the organ between his powerful mandibles. Spinning in place, he pushed through the mages led by Rugga and placed the tongue into the sundered oral cavity of his friend.

"It is yours by right," Krek said softly. "Yours is the destiny we must all follow and aid. Use the magic to heal yourself. Do it, friend Lan Martak. We need you!"

A tear formed at the corner of his saucer-sized eye. Inyx gently wiped it away as she hugged one of his thick middle legs and watched.

For minutes nothing happened; then Rugga jerked back, a look of surprise on her face.

"Our magics are blocked. We can no longer aid him. He . . . he is healing himself."

Inyx dared to hope then. More minutes passed and a startling transformation began. What had been bone once in Lan's face became bone again. Whitely exposed, it gleamed in the pale light of the setting sun. Then it was no longer visible. Skin flowed and covered it, recreating Lan's normal visage. But the young mage lay as still as death.

"Help him now," urged Inyx. "Give him your strength."

"He blocks us. All of us together cannot pierce the curtain he pulls about himself."

Then came the faint and eerie chants from Lan's newly grown lips. The spell mounted in power, built and soared to the skies. It was a spell of power and hope and success.

His eyes flickered open and soft brown eyes met Inyx's vivid blue ones.

"Lan?" she said hesitantly, unsure of herself, unsure of Lan.

"It'll be all right. The tongue. It . . . it's giving me power I never thought possible. The spells I only half-understood. They're crystal clear to me now. And more! I see so much more!"

Turning to Rugga, Inyx asked, "What effect will that tongue have on him? When Iron Tongue confronted Claybore, it drove him mad. Because the tongue was once Claybore's, might that not happen with Lan, also?"

All Rugga could do was shrug. She was the most potent sorcerer in Wurnna now and this was far beyond her expertise. Compared with Claybore—and Lan Martak—she was only an apprentice.

"While Murrk and his doughty warriors have routed the grey-clad army, Claybore still remains," pointed out Krek. "From what the skull has said, victory on this world is minor. Should not our attentions be directed elsewhere?"

"Claybore remains on this world," Lan said. "I 'feel' him nearby. If he is stopped now, the war is won." He got to his feet with Inyx's strong arm around his shoulders for support. He tapped into the power stone around him, allowed the tongue to roll in his mouth, be drenched with his saliva, become a part of his body—and soul.

"He still wants the tongue," said Jacy Noratumi.

"But now we can fight him for it. You can do it, Martak. You can!"

Lan said nothing. He waited, consolidating the power building within, savoring the richness of his senses, the nearness of his own death. When Claybore came, he was ready.

"The tongue!" demanded Claybore.

"Your death," said Lan in a voice so soft it was barely audible. But he did not merely speak, he used the Voice. "I want you to slay yourself. Kill yourself, Claybore. Die, *die!*" He put all the urgency possible into that command.

And Claybore started to obey.

Only a faint human voice crying out broke the spell and saved Claybore's quasi-existence.

The sorcerer trembled all over, shaking down to the mechanical legs bearing him.

"You have my tongue. You shall pay for this insult, Martak. You will wish you had died from my sword!"

Again came the human voice, clearer now, distinct and belonging to Kiska k'Adesina.

"All is ready, Master. Hurry. We must go. Patriccan can hold them back no longer. The troops are mutinying."

Claybore once more turned his attentions to Lan Martak. "I told your bitch. I tell you. This only seems victory for you. On other worlds, I have triumphed. When next we meet, do not think the battle will be so gentle."

Lan formed the most potent spell he knew and sent the bolt of energy blazing for Claybore. The leading edge of the energy spear wavered for an instant, then found only emptiness.

"Claybore has shifted worlds," moaned Inyx. "He has walked the Road."

"And there aren't any cenotaphs nearby," said Krek. "I 'see' one within a month's travel time, and I am not sure where that one leads. It might be onto another

world, altogether different from the one chosen by
Claybore.''

''If we don't hurry and follow him, he'll regain arms
and legs and become too powerful, even for you, Lan.''

''A cenotaph,'' mused the young mage. ''We can
create one out there, on the plain in front of Wurnna.''

''I suppose there are some bodies lost, but don't you
need to know the name for the consecration? It'll take
weeks to determine who has died and which corpses are
which. Oh, Lan, that'll take as long as hiking to the
cenotaph Krek 'sees.' ''

''We think in terms far too narrow. What to us is a
hero is to our enemies a villain.''

''So?''

''It is true the other way, also. A villain to us is a
hero to our enemies.''

''I don't see—no, Lan. You can't do this. I *hate*
him. I was angry when you denied me the chance to kill
him.''

''You would consecrate a cenotaph to Alberto Silvain?''
asked Krek. ''What a novel idea.''

''There is more to it than novelty, Krek. Silvain's
fortunes were linked with Claybore's. Properly done,
the cenotaph will continue to link their fortunes, and
this world with the one chosen by Claybore. It is the
only way we have of finding him among the myriad
worlds along the Road.''

Rugga stood, looking perplexed. For Jacy Noratumi's
part, he had no idea at all what the others argued over.
But both had arms around the other. The fortunes of
two destroyed cities, Bron and Wurnna, were now as
one.

Lan Martak left them behind to walk slowly to the
edge of the black pit he had formed. Into this vortex of
darkness Silvain had fallen. The flames of his life had
been snuffed out for all eternity and his body irretriev-
ably lost in a fashion that not even Lan Martak

understood. Perhaps the all-knowing Resident of the Pit might have been able to trace Silvain's course through the universe, but the Resident resided on Lan's home world, many worlds away.

Lan's hand rested on the closed grimoire he carried within his tunic. After a moment's pause, he knew he had no need to refresh his memory about the summoning spell or the proper method of consecration.

He began the chant, now surprisingly easy when uttered with the tongue that had once belonged to Claybore.

Inyx waved to Rugga and Noratumi as they stood in the wrecked gateway leading to the ruins of Wurnna. Then she turned and waved to the tiny dot on the top of the distant mountaintop. She thought the speck waved a furred leg in response, but she wasn't certain. Murrk and the humans remaining had come to an uneasy truce, but one which would grow into trust.

"Will the spiders honor the treaty?" she asked.

Lan didn't answer. Krek did.

"Murrk is honorable. He is Webmaster, after all. And if Jacy and Rugga keep the dam in fine repair and keep the stream in the valley to a mere trickle, there is no reason why Murrk will not allow mining of the power stone in his valley. It is all so simple now."

Krek turned and pointed with his long front leg. "The cenotaph opens."

"Silvain," muttered Inyx, remembering the foul deeds he had committed. But Lan had been correct. Silvain's courage in assuming the magical guise given by Claybore to attack an entire city filled with sorcerers had been strong enough to open the pathway between worlds.

"Ready?" asked Lan Martak.

"Is this truly the world where Claybore walks?"

The mage shrugged his shoulders. His powers had grown, but there were some—many—questions he had no answer for.

"Let us leave this fine world behind," said Krek. The spider boldly entered the simple stone cairn, wavered for a moment, and vanished from sight.

Lan Martak took Inyx's hand, squeezed it, and then led the way. They, too, shimmered as if caught in summer heat, felt the gut-wrenching shift to another world, then came out ready to pursue their adversary.

Claybore would not prevail. Not while they walked the Cenotaph Road.

MORE SCIENCE FICTION! ADVENTURE

BEST-SELLING
Science Fiction
and
Fantasy